The Robot Cried, "Help!"

Electronic entrepreneur Mike Gabriel was more than a little miffed when he found himself called back to active duty in Terra's space navy on the eve of a multimillion dollar business deal.

But when he was sent to a top-secret polar base without a word of explanation, his curiosity was aroused.

Then he heard what sounded like the voice of a woman or child calling for help from the sub-zero temperatures outside.

Plunging into the deadly cold, he comes face to face with a tall, looming form half-obscured by the snow.

He has just met Snookums, the most amazing robot ever built.

Snookums has the mind of a child and the power to destroy the world.

And Snookums is beginning to throw tantrums!

Also by Randall Garrett

EARTH INVADER   **LB1059-3**

STARSHIP
DEATH

Randall Garrett

LEISURE BOOKS  **NEW YORK CITY**

A LEISURE BOOK

Published by

Nordon Publications, Inc.
Two Park Avenue
New York, N.Y. 10016

Copyright © MCMLXII by Randall Garrett

Published by arrangement with the author's agent, Tracy
Blackstone, Inc.

STARSHIP
DEATH

INTRODUCTION

Most of the readers who have helped make Randall
Garrett's three Lord Darcy books science fiction best-
sellers have never heard of Jonathan Blake MacKenzie,
David Gordon, Walter Bupp, Mark Phillips or any of
the more than seventeen pseudonyms under which he
has also written in the field.

A prolific writer, until his recent illness, he had sold
so many stories to one high-paying editor, that he was
forced to resort to subterfuge, resulting in *Earth Invader,* another Randall Garrett book available in a Leisure edition.

He claims to have sold his first story to John W.
Campbell of "Astounding" when he was fourteen, but
a comparison of the dates indicates he was somewhat
older. Even so, seventeen is still an impressive age to
have made a debut in what was then acknowledged as
the best magazine in the field.

In the early 1950s he was one of a stable of "house
writers"—including Robert Silverberg, Milton Lesser,
Harlan Ellison, and Paul Fairman—for the Ziff-Davis

magazines, "Amazing" and "Fantastic," inheriting a situation created by Raymond Palmer.

Most of the pseudonyms under which Mr. Garrett has written reveal his sense of humor, such as Darrel T. Langert (which is an anagram of his own name), or Gordon Aghill (for a collaboration with Robert Silverberg).

This humor runs through all his published work, which is probably one reason for his popularity in a field which has, until recently, been all too serious.

His first big success was with the Kenneth Malone series for "Astounding."

He began with *That Sweet Little Old Lady* (later retitled *Braintwister*). It told of a harried near-future FBI agent and his attempts to deal with a variety of criminals possessing psychic powers, including an old woman telepath who thinks she is Queen Elizabeth I and he's Sir Walter Raleigh, and a kid gang that can teleport itself anywhere it wants.

The opening paragraphs of *The Shrouded Planet*, a more serious work, nevertheless slyly ape, as Robert Silverberg has pointed out, the narrative hooks of an earlier age's science fiction.

This sense of humor is equally evident in *Starship Death*. (In fact, *Star Trek* fans will find in it the inspiration for several of their favorite episodes and the climax of the new movie.)

Like all of Garrett's humor, it is the laughter of a man who sees all humanity's foibles and loves them anyway.

Like *Earth Invader*, it is a study in the psychology of an alien mind. In this case a robot mind.

Like that book, *Starship Death* is a fast-moving, action-adventure story set against a near-future background. It ends up in space and attempts to resolve important social issues.

Starship Death is also the only Garrett novel of the period not to have been serialized in "Analog."

This may have been the result of one of the jokes which Garrett liked to play on John Campbell in those days. In a recent article, science fiction author Algis Budrys revealed that, during the period when Campbell publicly tabulated readers' votes on each issue's stories and awarded a substantial bonus to the most popular, two writers tried to influence the results—one for financial gain, and one as a joke to see if it could really be done.

Campbell is supposed to have banished the former from his pages forever, and in time forgiven the latter.

Although Garrett refuses to confirm that he was the second of the two writers, neither will he not deny it.

That could be an admission, of course—or just another example of his playful sense of humor.

Hank Stine

1

The kids who tried to jump Mike the Angel were bright enough in a lot of ways, but they made a bad mistake when they tangled with Mike the Angel.

They'd done their preliminary work well enough. They had cased the job thoroughly, and they had built the equipment to take care of it. Their mistake was not in their planning; it was in not taking Mike the Angel into account.

There is a section of New York's Manhattan Island, down on the lower West Side, that has been known, for over a century, as "Radio Row." All through this section are stores, large and small, where every kind of electronic and sub-electronic device can be bought, ordered, or designed to order. There is even an old antique shop, known as Ye Quainte Olde Elecktronicks Shoppe, where you can buy such oddities as vacuum-tube FM radios and twenty-four-inch cathode-ray television sets. And, if you want them, transmitters to match, so you can watch the antiques work.

Mike the Angel had an uptown office in the heart of

the business district, near West 112th Street—a very posh suite of rooms on the fiftieth floor of the half-mile-high Timmins Building, overlooking the two-hundred-year-old Gothic edifice of the Cathedral of St. John the Divine. The glowing sign on the door of the suite said, very simply:

M. R. GABRIEL
POWER DESIGN

But, once or twice a week, Mike the Angel liked to take off and prowl around Radio Row, just shopping around. Usually, he didn't work too late, but, on this particular afternoon, he'd been in his office until after six o'clock, working on some papers for the Interstellar Commission. So, by the time he got down to Radio Row, the only shop left open was Harry MacDougal's.

That didn't matter much to Mike the Angel, since Harry's was the place he had intended to go, anyway. Harry MacDougal's establishment was hardly more than a hole in the wall—a narrow, long hallway between two larger stores. Although not a specialist, like the proprietor of Ye Quainte Olde Elecktronicks Shoppe, Harry did carry equipment of every vintage and every make. If you wanted something that hadn't been manufactured in decades, and perhaps never made in quantity, Harry's was the place to go. The walls were lined with bins, all unlabeled, filled helter-skelter with every imaginable kind of gadget, most of which would have been hard to recognize unless you were both an expert and a historian.

Old Harry didn't need labels or a system. He was a small, lean, bony, sharp-nosed Scot who had fled Scot-

12

land during the Panic of '37, landed in New York, and stopped. He solemnly declared that he had never been west of the Hudson River nor north of 181st Street in the more than fifty years he had been in the country. He had a mind like that of a robot filing cabinet. Ask him for a particular piece of equipment, and he'd squint one eye closed, stare at the end of his nose with the other, and say:

"An M-1993 thermodyne hexode, eh? Ah. Um. Aye, I got one. Picked it up a couple years back. Put it— Let ma see, now . . ."

And he'd go to his wall ladder, push it along that narrow hallway, moving boxes aside as he went, and stop somewhere along the wall. Then he'd scramble up the ladder, pull out a bin, fumble around in it, and come out with the article in question. He'd blow the dust off it, polish it with a rag, scramble down the ladder, and say: "Here 'tis. Thought I had one. Let's go back in the back and give her a test."

On the other hand, if he didn't have what you wanted, he'd shake his head just a trifle, then squint up at you and say: "What d'ye want it for?" And if you could tell him what you planned to do with the piece you wanted, nine times out of ten he could come up with something else that would do the job as well or better.

In either case, he always insisted that the piece be tested. He refused either to buy or sell something that didn't work. So you'd follow him down that long hallway to the lab in the rear, where all the testing equipment was. The lab, too, was cluttered, but in a different way. Out front, the stuff was dead; back here, there was power coursing through the ionic veins and metallic nerves of the half-living machines. Things were labeled

13

in neat, accurate script—not for Old Harry's benefit, but for the edification of his customers, so they wouldn't put their fingers in the wrong places. He never had to worry about whether his customers knew enough to fend for themselves; a few minutes spent in talking was enough to tell Harry whether a man knew enough about the science and art of electronics and sub-electronics to be trusted in the lab. If you didn't measure up, you didn't get invited to the lab, even to watch a test.

But he had very few people like that; nobody came into Harry MacDougal's place unless he was pretty sure of what he wanted and how he wanted to use it.

On the other hand, there were very few men whom Harry would allow into the lab unescorted. Mike the Angel was one of them.

Meet Mike the Angel. Full name: Michael Raphael Gabriel. (His mother had tagged that on him at the time of his baptism, which had made his father wince in anticipated compassion, but there had been nothing for him to say—not in the middle of the ceremony.)

Naturally, he had been tagged "Mike the Angel." Six feet seven. Two hundred sixty pounds. Thirty-four years of age. Hair: golden yellow. Eyes: deep blue. Cash value of holdings: well into eight figures. Credit: almost unlimited. Marital status: highly eligible, if the right woman could tackle him.

Mike the Angel pushed open the door to Harry Mac-Dougal's shop and took off his hat to brush the rain-drops from it. Farther uptown, the streets were covered with clear plastic roofing, but that kind of comfort stopped at Fifty-third Street.

There was no one in sight in the long, narrow store, so

14

Mike the Angel looked up at the ceiling, where he knew the eye was hidden.

"Harry?" he said.

"I see you, lad," said a voice from the air. "You got here just in time. I'm closin' up. Lock the door, would ye?"

"Sure, Harry." Mike turned around, pressed the locking switch, and heard it snap satisfactorily.

"Okay, Mike," said Harry MacDougal's voice. "Come on back. I hope ye brought that bottle of scotch I asked for."

Mike the Angel made his way back between the towering tiers of bins as he answered. "Sure did, Harry. When did I ever forget you?"

And, as he moved toward the rear of the store, Mike the Angel casually reached into his coat pocket and triggered the switch of a small but fantastically powerful mechanism that he always carried when he walked the streets of New York at night.

He was headed straight into trouble, and he knew it. And he hoped he was ready for it.

2

Mike the Angel kept his hand in his pocket, his thumb on a little plate that was set in the side of the small mechanism that was concealed therein. As he neared the door, the little plate began to vibrate, making a buzz which could only be felt, not heard. Mike sighed to himself. Vibroblades were all the rage this season.

He pushed open the rear door rapidly and stepped inside. It was just what he'd expected. His eyes saw and his brain recorded the whole scene in the fraction of a second before he moved. In that fraction of a second, he took in the situation, appraised it, planned his strategy, and launched into his plan of action.

Harry MacDougal was sitting at his workbench, near the controls of the eye that watched the shop when he was in the lab. He was hunched over a little, his small, bright eyes peering steadily at Mike the Angel from beneath shaggy, silvered brows. There was no pleading in those eyes—only confidence.

Next to Old Harry was a kid—sixteen, maybe seventeen. He had the JD stamp on his face: a look of cold, hard arrogance that barely concealed the uncertainty and fear beneath. One hand was at Harry's back, and Mike knew that the kid was holding a vibroblade at the old man's spine.

At the same time, the buzzing against his thumb told Mike the Angel something else. There was a vibroblade much nearer his body than the one in the kid's hand.

That meant that there was another young punk behind him.

All this took Mike the Angel about one quarter of a second to assimilate. Then he jumped.

Had the intruders been adults, Mike would have handled the entire situation in a completely different way. Adults, unless they are mentally or emotionally retarded, do not usually react or behave like children. Adolescents can, do, and *must*—for the very simple reason that they have not yet had time to learn to react as adults.

Had the intruders been adults, and had Mike the Angel behaved the way he did, he might conceivably have died that night. As it was, the kids never had a chance.

Mike didn't even bother to acknowledge the existence of the punk behind him. He leaped, instead, straight for the kid in the dead-black suede zipsuit who was holding the vibroblade against Harry MacDougal's spine. And the kid reacted exactly as Mike the Angel had hoped, prayed, and predicted he would.

The kid defended himself.

An adult, in a situation where he has one known enemy at his mercy and is being attacked by a second, will quickly put the first out of the way in order to leave himself free to deal with the second. There is no sense in leaving your flank wide open just to oppose a frontal attack.

If the kid had been an adult, Harry MacDougal would have died there and then. An adult would simply have slashed his vibroblade through the old man's spine and brought it to bear on Mike the Angel.

But not the kid. He jumped back, eyes widening, to face his oncoming opponent in an open space. He was no coward,that kid, and he knew how to handle a vibroblade. In his own unwise, suicidal way, he was perfectly capable of proving himself. He held out the point of that shimmering metal shaft, ready to parry any offensive thrust that Mike the Angel might make.

If Mike had had a vibroblade himself, and if there hadn't been another punk at his back, Mike might have taken care of the kid that way. As it was, he had no choice but to use another way.

He threw himself full on the point of the scintillating vibroblade.

A vibroblade is a nasty weapon. Originally designed as a surgeon's tool, its special steel blade moves in and out of the heavy hilt at speeds from two hundred to two thousand vibrations per second, depending on the size and the use to which it is to be put. Make it eight inches long, add serrated, diamond-pointed teeth, and you have the man-killing vibroblade. Its danger is in its power; that shivering blade can cut through flesh, cartilage, and bone with almost no effort. It's a knife with power steering.

But that kind of power can be a weakness as well as a strength.

The little gadget that Mike the Angel carried did more than just detect the nearby operation of a vibroblade. It was also a defense. The gadget focused a high-density magnetic field on any vibroblade that came anywhere within six inches of Mike's body.

In that field, the steel blade simply couldn't move. It was as though it had been caught in a vise. The blade no longer vibrated; it had become nothing more than an overly fancy bread knife.

The trouble was that the power unit in the heavy hilt simply wouldn't accept the fact that the blade was immovable. That power unit was in there to move something, and by heaven, *something* had to move.

The hilt jerked and bucked in the kid's hand, taking skin with it. Then it began to smoke and burn under the overload. The plastic shell cracked and hot copper and silver splattered out of it. The kid screamed as the molten metal burned his hand.

Mike the Angel put a hand against the kid's chest and shoved. As the boy toppled backward, Mike turned to face the other boy.

Only it wasn't a boy.

She was wearing gold lip paint and had sprayed her hair blue, but she knew how to handle a vibroblade at least as well as her boy friend had. Just as Mike the Angel turned, she lunged forward, aiming for the small of his back.

And she, too, screamed as she lost her blade in a flash of heat.

Then she grabbed for something in her pocket. Regretfully, Mike the Angel brought the edge of his hand down against the side of her neck in a paralyzing, but not deadly, rabbit punch. She dropped, senseless, and a small gun spilled out of the waist pocket of her zipsuit and skittered across the floor. Mike paused only long enough to make sure she was out, then he turned back to his first opponent.

As he had anticipated, Harry MacDougal had taken charge. The kid was sprawled flat on the floor, and Old Harry was holding a shock gun in his hand.

Mike the Angel took a deep breath.

"Yer trousers are on fire," said Harry.

Mike yelped as he felt the heat, and he began slapping at the smoldering spots where the molten metal from the vibroblades had hit his clothing. He wasn't afire; modern clothing doesn't flame up—but it can get pretty hot when you splash liquid copper on it.

"Damn!" said Mike the Angel. "New suit, too."

"You're a fast thinker, laddie," said Old Harry.

"You don't need to flatter me, Harry," said Mike the Angel. "When an old teetotaler like you asks a man if he's brought some scotch, the man's a fool if he doesn't know there's trouble afoot." He gave his leg a final slap and said: "What happened? Are there any more of them?"

"Don't know. Might be." The old man waved at his control panel. "My instruments are workin' again!" He gestured at the floor. "I'm nae sure how they did it, but somehow they managed to blank out ma instruments just long enough to get inside. Their mistake was in not lockin' the front door."

Mike the Angel was busy searching the two unconscious kids. He looked up. "Neither of them is carrying any equipment in their clothing—at least, not anything that's self-powered. If they've got pickup circuits built into the cloth, there must be more of them outside."

"Aye. Likely. We'll see."

Suddenly, there was a soft *ping! ping! ping!* from an instrument on the bench.

Harry glanced quickly at the receiving screen that was connected with the multitude of eyes that were hidden around the area of his shop. Then a smile came over his small brown face.

"Cops," he said. "Time they got here."

3

Sergeant Cowder looked the room over and took a drag from his cigarette. "Well, that's that. Now—what happened?" He looked from Mike the Angel to Harry MacDougal and back again. Both of them appeared to be thinking.

"All right," he said quietly, "let me guess, then."

Old Harry waved a hand. "Oh no, Sergeant; 'twon't be necessary. I think Mr. Gabriel was just waiting for me to start, because he wasn't here when the two rapscallions came in, and I was just tryin' to figure out where to begin. We're not bein' unco-operative. Let's see now—" He gazed at the ceiling as though trying to collect his thoughts. He knew perfectly well that the police sergeant was recording everything he said.

The sergeant sighed. "Look, Harry, you're not on trial. I know perfectly well that you've got this place bugged to a fare-thee-well. So does every shop operator on Radio Row. If you didn't, the JD gangs would have cleaned you all out long ago."

Harry kept looking at the ceiling, and Mike the Angel smiled quietly at his fingernails.

The detective sergeant sighed again. "Sure, we'd like to have some of the gadgets that you and the other operators on the Row have worked out, Harry. But I'm in no position to take 'em away from you. Besides, we have some stuff that you'd like to have, too, so that makes us pretty much even. If we started confiscating illegal equipment from you, the JD's would swoop in here, take your legitimate equipment, bug it up, and they'd be driving us all nuts within a week. So long as you don't use illegal equipment illegally, the department will leave you alone."

Old Harry grinned. "Well, now, that's very nice of you, Sergeant. But I don't have anything illegal—no robotics stuff or anything like that. Oh, I'll admit I've a couple of eyes here and there to watch my shop, but eyes aren't illegal."

The detective glanced around the room with a practiced eye and then looked blandly back at the little Scotsman. Harry MacDougal was lying, and the sergeant knew it. And Harry knew the sergeant knew it.

Sergeant Cowder sighed for a third time and looked at the Scot. "Okay. So what happened?"

Harry's face became serious. "They came in about six-thirty. First I knew of it, one of the kids—the boy—stepped out of that closet over there and put a vibroblade at my back. I'd come back here to get a small resistor, and all of a sudden there he was."

Mike the Angel frowned, but he didn't say anything.

"None of your equipment registered anything?" asked the detective.

"Not a thing, Sergeant," said Harry. "They've got something new, all right. The kid must ha' come in through the back door, there. And I'd ha' been willin'

24

to bet ma life that no human bein' could ha' walked in here without ma knowin' it before he got within ten feet o' tnat door. Look.''

He got up, walked over to the back door, and opened it. It opened into what looked at first to be a totally dark room. Then the sergeant saw that there was a dead-black wall a few feet from the open door.

"That's a light trap," said Harry. "Same as they have in photographic darkrooms. To get from this door to the outer door that leads into the alley, you got to turn two corners and walk about thirty feet. Even I, masel', couldn't walk through it without settin' off half a dozen alarms. Any kind of light would set off the bugs; so would the heat radiation from the human body.''

"How about the front?" Sergeant Cowder asked. "Anyone could get in from the front."

Harry's grin became grim. "Not unless I go with 'em. And not even then if I don't want 'em to."

"It was kind of you to let *us* in," said the detective mildly.

"A pleasure," said Harry. "But I wish I knew how that kid got in."

"Well, he did—somehow," Cowder said. "What happened after he came out of the closet?"

"He made me let the girl in. They were goin' to open up the rear completely and take my stuff out that way. They'd ha' done it, too, if Mr. Gabriel hadn't come along."

Detective Sergeant Cowder looked at Mike the Angel. "About what time was that, Mr. Gabriel?"

"About six thirty-five," Mike told him. "The kids probably hadn't been here more than a few minutes."

Harry MacDougal nodded in silent corroboration.

"Then what happened?" asked the detective.

Mike told him a carefully edited version of what had occurred, leaving out the existence of the little gadget he was carrying in his pocket. The sergeant listened patiently and unbelievingly through the whole recital. Mike the Angel grinned to himself; he knew what part of the story seemed queer to the cop.

He was right. Cowder said: "Now, wait a minute. What caused those vibroblades to burn up that way?"

"Must have been faulty," Mike the Angel said innocently.

"Both of them?" Sergeant Cowder asked skeptically. "At the same time?"

"Oh no. Thirty seconds apart, I'd guess."

"Very interesting. Very." He started to say something else, but a uniformed officer stuck his head in through the doorway that led to the front of the shop.

"We combed the whole area, Sergeant. Not a soul around. But from the looks of the alley, there must have been a small truck parked in there not too long ago."

Cowder nodded. "Makes sense. Those JD's wouldn't have tried this unless they intended to take everything they could put their hands on, and they certainly couldn't have put all this in their pockets." He rubbed one big finger over the tip of his nose. "Okay, Barton, that's all. Take those two kids to the hospital and book 'em in the detention ward. I want to talk to them when they wake up."

The cop nodded and left.

Sergeant Cowder looked back at Harry. "Your alarm to the precinct station went off at six thirty-six. I figure that whoever was on the outside, in that truck, knew something had gone wrong as soon as the fight started in here. He—or they—shut off whatever they were using to suppress the alarm system and took off before we got here. They sure must have moved fast."

"Must have," agreed Harry. "Is there anything else, Sergeant?"

Cowder shook his head. "Not right now. I'll get in touch with you later, if I need you."

Harry and Mike the Angel followed him through the front of the shop to the front door. At the door, Cowder turned.

"Well, good night. Thanks for your assistance, Mr. Gabriel. I wish some of our cops had had your luck."

"How so?" asked Mike the Angel.

"If more vibroblades would blow up at opportune moments, we'd have fewer butchered policemen."

Mike the Angel shook his head. "Not really. If their vibros started burning out every time they came near a cop, the JD's would just start using something else. You can't win in this game."

Cowder nodded glumly. "It's a losing proposition any way you look at it . . . Well, good night again." He stepped out, and Old Harry closed and locked the door behind him.

Mike the Angel said: "Come on, Harry; I want to find something." He began walking back down the long, narrow shop toward the rear again. Harry followed, looking mystified.

Mike the Angel stopped, sniffing. "Smell that?"

Harry sniffed. "Aye. Burnt insulation. So?"

"You know which one of these bins is nearest to your main control cable. Start looking. See if you find anything queer."

Old Harry walked over to a nearby bin, pulled it open, and looked inside. He closed it, pulled open another. He found the gadget on the third try. It was a plastic case, six by six by eight, and it still smelled of hot insulation, although the case itself was barely warm.

"What is it?" Harry asked in wonder.

"It's the gizmo that turned your equipment off. When I passed by it, my own gadget must have blown it. I knew the police couldn't have made it here between the time of the fight and the time they showed up. They must have had at least an extra minute. Besides, I didn't think anyone could build an instrument that would blank out everything at long range. It had to be something near your main cable. I think you'll find a metallic oscillator in there. Analyze it. Might be useful."

Harry turned the box over in his hands. "Probably has a timer in it to start it . . . Well . . . That helps."

"What do you mean?"

"I've got a pretty good idea who put it here: Older kid. Nineteen—maybe twenty. Seemed like a nice lad, too. Didn't take him for a JD. Can't trust anyone these days. Thanks, Mike. If I find anything new in here, I'll let you know."

"Do that," said Mike the Angel. "And, as a personal favor, I'll show you how to build my own super-duper, extra-special, anti-vibroblade defense unit."

Old Harry grinned, crinkling up his wizened face in a mass of fine wrinkles. "You'd better think up a shorter name than that for it, laddie; I could probably build one in less time than it takes you to say it."

"Want to bet?"

"I'll bet you twenty I can do it in twenty-four hours."

"Twenty it is, Harry. I'll sell you mine this time

28

tomorrow for twenty bucks."

Harry shook his head. "I'll trade you mine for yours, plus twenty." Then his eyes twinkled. "And speaking of money, didn't you come down here to buy something?"

Mike the Angel laughed. "You're not going to like it. I came down to get a dozen plastic-core resistors."

"What size?"

Mike told him, and Old Harry went over to the proper bin, pulled them out, all properly boxed, and handed them to him.

"That'll be four dollars," he said.

Mike the Angel paid up with a smile. "You don't happen to have a hundred-thousand-unit microcryotron stack, do you?"

"Ain't s'posed to," said Harry MacDougal. "If I did, I wouldn't sell it to you. But, as a matter of cold fact, I do happen to have one. Use it for a paperweight. I'll give it to you for nothing, because it don't work, anyhow."

"Maybe I can fix it," said Mike the Angel, "as long as you're giving it to me. How come it doesn't work?"

"Just a second, laddie," said Harry. He scuttled to the rear of the shop and came back with a ready-wrapped package measuring five by five by four. He handed it to Mike the Angel and said: "It's a present. Thanks for helping me out of a tight spot."

Mike said something deprecative of his own efforts and took the package. If it were in working order it would have been worth close to three hundred dollars—more than that on the black market. If it was broken, though, it was no good to Mike. A microcryotron unit is almost impossible to fix if it breaks down. But Mike took it because he didn't want to hurt Old

29

Harry's feelings by refusing a present.

"Thanks, Harry," he said. "Happen to know why it doesn't work?"

Harry's face crinkled again in his all-over smile. "Sure, Mike. It ain't plugged in."

4

Mike the Angel did not believe in commuting. Being a bachelor, he could afford to indulge in that belief. In his suite of offices on 112th Street, there was one door marked "Mr. R. Gabriel." Behind that door was his private secretary's office, which acted as an effective barrier between himself and the various employees of the firm. Behind the secretary's office was his own office.

There was still another door in his inner office, a plain, unmarked door that looked as though it might conceal a closet.

It didn't. It was the door to a veddy, veddy expensive apartment with equally expensive appointments. One wall, thirty feet long and ten feet high, was a nearly invisible, dustproof slab of polished, optically flat glass that gave the observer the feeling that there was nothing between him and the city street, five hundred feet below.

The lights of the city, coming through the wall, gave the room plenty of illumination after sunset, but the

31

simple flick of a switch could polarize it black, allowing perfect privacy.

The furniture was massive, heavily braced, and well upholstered. It had to be; Mike the Angel liked to flop into chairs, and his two hundred and sixty pounds gave chairs a lot of punishment.

On one of the opaque walls was Dali's original "Eucharist," with its muffled, robed figures looking oddly luminous in the queer combination of city lights and interior illumination. Farther back, a Valois gleamed metallically above the shadowed bas-reliefs of its depths.

It was the kind of apartment Mike the Angel liked. He could sleep, if necessary, on a park bench or in a trench, but he didn't see any reason for doing so if he could sleep on a five-hundred-dollar floater.

As he had passed through each door, he had checked them carefully. His electrokey had a special circuit that lighted up a tiny glow lamp in the key handle if the lock had been tampered with. None of them had.

He opened the final door, went into his apartment, and locked the door behind him, as he had locked the others. Then he turned on the lights, peeled off his raincoat, and plopped himself into a chair to unwrap the microcryotron stack he had picked up at Harry's.

Theoretically, Harry wasn't supposed to sell the things. They were still difficult to make, and they were supposed to be used only by persons who were authorized to build robot brains, since that's what the stack was—a part of a robot brain. Mike could have put his hands on one legally, provided he'd wanted to wait for six or eight months to clear up the red tape. Actually, the big robotics companies didn't want amateurs fooling around with robots; they'd much rather build the robots themselves and rent them out. They couldn't make do-it-yourself projects impossible, but they could make them difficult.

In a way, there was some good done. So far, the JD's hadn't gone into big-scale robotics. Self-controlled bombs could be rather nasty.

Adult criminals, of course, already had them. But an adult criminal who had the money to invest in robotic components, or went to the trouble to steal them, had something more lucrative in mind than street fights or robbing barrooms. To crack a bank, for instance, took a cleverly constructed, well-designed robot and plenty of ingenuity on the part of the operator.

Mike the Angel didn't want to make bombs or automatic bankrobbers; he just wanted to fiddle with the stack, see what it would do. He turned it over in his hands a couple of times, then shrugged, got up, went over to his closet, and put the thing away. There wasn't anything he could do with it until he'd bought a cryostat—a liquid helium refrigerator. A cryotron functions only at temperatures near absolute zero.

The phone chimed.

Mike went over to it, punched the switch, and said: "Gabriel speaking."

No image formed on the screen. A voice said: "Sorry, wrong number." There was a slight click, and the phone went dead. Mike shrugged and punched the cutoff. Sounded like a woman. He vaguely wished he could have seen her face.

Mike got up and walked back to his easy chair. He had no sooner sat down than the phone chimed again. Damn!

Up again. Back to the phone.

"Gabriel speaking."

Again, no image formed.

"Look, lady," Mike said, "why don't you look up the number you want instead of bothering me?"

Suddenly there was an image. It was the face of an elderly man with a mild, reddish face, white hair, and a cold look in his pale blue eyes. It was Basil Wallingford, the Minister for Spatial Affairs.

He said: "Mike, I wasn't aware that your position was such that you could afford to be rude to a Portfolio of the Earth Government." His voice was flat, without either anger or humor.

"I'm not sure it is, myself," admitted Mike the Angel, "but I do the best I can with the tools I have to work with. I didn't know it was you, Wally. I just had some wrong-number trouble. Sorry."

"Mf . . . Well . . . I called to tell you that the *Branchell* is ready for your final inspection. Or will be, that is, in a week."

"My final inspection?" Mike the Angel arched his heavy golden-blond eyebrows. "Hell, Wally, Serge Paulvitch is on the job down there, isn't he? You don't need *my* okay. If Serge says it's ready to go, it's ready to go. Or is there some kind of trouble you haven't mentioned yet?"

"No; no trouble," said Wallingford. "But the power plant on that ship was built according to your designs—not Mr. Paulvitch's. The Bureau of Space feels that you should give them the final check."

Mike knew when to argue and when not to, and he knew that this was one time when it wouldn't do him the slightest good. "All right," he said resignedly. "I don't like Antarctica and never will, but I guess I can stand it for a few days."

"Fine. One more thing. Do you have a copy of the thrust specifications for Cargo Hold One? Our copy got garbled in transmission, and there seems to be a discrepancy in the figures."

Mike nodded. "Sure. They're in my office. Want me to get them now?"

"Please. I'll hold on."

Mike the Angel barely made it in time. He went to the door that led to his office, opened it, stepped through, and closed it behind him just as the blast went off.

The door shuddered behind Mike, but it didn't give. Mike's apartment was reasonably soundproof, but it wasn't built to take the kind of explosion that would shake the door that Mike the Angel had just closed. It was a two-inch-thick slab of armor steel on heavy, precision-bearing hinges. So was every other door in the suite. It wasn't quite a bank-vault door, but it would do. Any explosion that could shake it was a real doozy.

Mike the Angel spun around and looked at the door. It was just a trifle warped, and faint tendrills of vapor were curling around the edge where the seal had been broken. Mike sniffed, then turned and ran. He opened a drawer in his desk and took out a big roll of electrostatic tape. Then he took a deep breath, went back to the door, and slapped on a strip of the one-inch tape, running it all around the edge of the door. Then he went into the outer office while the air conditioners cleaned out his private office.

He went over to one of the phones near the autofile and punched for the operator. "I had a long-distance call coming in here from the Right Excellent Basil

Wallingford, Minister for Spatial Affairs, Capitol City. We were cut off."

"One moment please." A slight pause. "His Excellency is here, Mr. Gabriel."

Wallingford's face came back on the screen. It had lost some of its ruddiness. "What happened?" he asked.

"You tell me, Wally," Mike snapped. "Did you see anything at all?"

"All I saw was that big pane of glass break. It fell into a thousand pieces, and then something exploded and the phone went dead."

"The glass broke first?"

"That's right."

Mike sighed. "Good. I was afraid that maybe someone had planted that bomb, rather than fired it in. I'd hate to think anyone could get into my place without my knowing it."

"Who's gunning for you?"

"I wish I knew. Look, Wally, can you wait until tomorrow for those specs? I want to get hold of the police."

"Certainly. Nothing urgent. It can wait. I'll call you again tomorrow evening." The screen blanked.

Mike glanced at the wall clock and then punched a number on the phone. A pretty girl in a blue uniform came on the screen.

"Police Central," she said. "May I help you?"

"I'd like to speak to Detective Sergeant William Cowder, please," Mike said. "Just tell him that Mr. Gabriel has more problems."

She looked puzzled, but she nodded, and pretty soon her image blanked out. The screen stayed blank, but

Sergeant Cowder's voice came over the speaker. "What is it, Mr. Gabriel?"

He was evidently speaking from a pocket phone.

"Attempted murder," said Mike the Angel. "A few minutes ago a bomb was set off in my apartment. I think it was a rocket, and I know it was heavily laced with hydrogen cyanide. That's Suite 5000, Timmins Building, up on 112th Street. I called you because I have a hunch it's connected with the incident at Harry's earlier this evening."

"Timmins Building, eh? I'll be right up."

Cowder cut off with a sharp click, and Mike the Angel looked quizzically at the dead screen. Was he imagining things, or was there a peculiar note in Cowder's voice?

Two minutes later he got his answer.

5

Mike the Angel was sitting behind his desk in his private office when the announcer chimed. Mike narrowed his eyes and turned on his door screen, which connected with an eye in the outer door of the suite. Who could it be this time?

It was Sergeant Cowder.

"You got here fast," said Mike, thumbing the unlocker. "Come on back to my office."

The sergeant came through the outer office while Mike watched him on the screen. Not until the officer finally pushed open the door to Mike's own office did Mike the Angel look up from the screen.

"I repeat," said Mike, "you got here fast."

"I wasn't far away," said Cowder. "Where's the damage?"

Mike jerked a thumb toward the door to his apartment, still sealed with tape. "In there."

"Have you been back in there yet?"

"Nope," said Mike. "I didn't want to disturb anything. I figured maybe your lab boys could tell where the rocket came from."

"What happened?" the cop asked.

Mike told him, omitting nothing except the details of his conversation with Wallingford.

"The way I see it," he finished, "whoever it was phoned me to make sure I was in the room and then went out and fired a rocket at my window."

"What makes you think it was a JD?" Cowder said.

"Well, Sergeant, if I were going to do the job, I'd put my launcher in some place where I could see that my victim was inside, without having to call him. But if I couldn't do that, I'd aim the launcher and set it to fire by remote control. Then I'd go to the phone, call him, and fire the rocket while he was on the phone. I'd be sure of getting him that way. The way it was done smacks of a kid's trick."

Cowder looked at the door. "Think we can go in there now? The HCN ought to have cleared out by now."

Mike stood up from behind his desk. "I imagine it's pretty clear. I checked the air conditioners; they're still working, and the filters are efficient enough to take care of an awful lot of hydrogen cyanide. Besides, the window is open. But—shouldn't we wait for the lab men?"

Cowder shook his head. "Not necessary. They'll be up in a few minutes, but they'll probably just confirm what we already know. Peel that tape off, will you?"

Mike took his ionizer from the top of the desk, walked over to the door, and began running it over the tape. It fell off and slithered to the floor. As he worked, he said:

"You think you know where the rocket was fired from?"

"Almost positive," said Cowder. "We got a call a few minutes back from the Cathedral of St. John the Divine."

The last of the tape fell off, and Mike opened the door. It didn't work easily, but it did open. The odor of bitter almonds was so faint that it might actually have been imagination.

Cowder pointed out the shattered window at the gray spire of the cathedral. "There's your launching site. We don't know how they got up there, but they managed."

"They?"

"Two of them. When they tried to leave, a couple of priests and two officers of the Cathedral Police spotted them. The kids dropped their launcher and two unfired rockets, and then tried to run for it. Result: one dead kid, one getaway. One of the cops got a bad gash on his arm from a vibroblade, and one of the priests got it in the abdomen. He'll live, but he's in bad shape."

Mike said something under his breath that might have been an oath, except that it avoided all mention of the Deity. Then he added that Name, in a different tone of voice.

"I agree," said Cowder. "You think you know why they did it?"

Mike looked around at his apartment. At first glance it appeared to be a total loss, but closer inspection showed that most of the damage had been restricted to glass and ceramics. The furniture had been tumbled around but not badly damaged. The war head of the rocket had evidently been of the concussion-and-gas type, without much fragmentation.

"I think I know why, yes," Mike said, turning back to the sergeant. "I had a funny feeling all the way home from Harry's. Nothing I could lay my finger on, really. I tried to see if I was being followed, but I didn't spot anyone. There were plenty of kids on the subway.

"It's my guess that the kids knew who I was. If they cased Harry's as thoroughly as it seems they did, they must have seen me go in and out several times. They knew that it was my fault that two of their members got picked up, so they decided to teach me a lesson. One of them must have come up here, even before I left Harry's. The other followed me, just to make sure I was really coming home. Since he knew where I was going, he didn't have to stick too close, so I didn't spot him in the crowd. He might even have gone on up to 116th Street so that I wouldn't see him get off at 110th."

"Sounds reasonable," Cowder agreed. "We know who the kids are. The uniformed squads are rounding up the whole bunch for questioning. They call themselves—you'll get a laugh out of this!—they call themselves the Rocketeers."

"I'm fracturing my funny bone," said Mike the Angel. "The thing that gets me is this revenge business, though. Kids don't usually go that far out for fellow gang members."

"Not usually," the sergeant said, "but this is a little different. The girl you caught and the boy who got killed over at the cathedral are brother and sister."

"That explains it," Mike said. "Rough family, eh?"

Sergeant Cowder shook his head. "Not really. The parents are respectable and fairly well off. Larchmont's the name. The kids are Susan and Herbert—Sue and Bert to you. Bert's sixteen, Sue's seventeen. They were pretty thick, I gather: real brother and sister team."

"Good family, bad kids," Mike muttered. He had wandered over to the wall to look at his Dali. It had fallen to the floor, but it wasn't hurt. The Valois was bent, but it could be fixed up easily enough.

"I wonder," Mike said, picking up the head of a smashed figurine and looking at it. "I wonder if the so-called sociologists have any explanation for it?"

"Sure," Cowder said. "Same one they've been giving for more decades than I'd care to think of. The mother was married before. Divorced her husband, married Larchmont. But she had a boy by her first husband."

"Broken home and sibling rivalry? *Pfui*! And if it wasn't that, the sociologists would find another excuse," Mike said angrily.

"Funny thing is that the older half brother was a perfectly respectable kid. Made good grades in school, joined the Space Service, has a perfectly clean record. And yet *he* was the product of the broken home, not the two younger kids."

Mike laughed dryly. "*That* ought to be food for high sociological thought."

The door announcer chimed again, and Cowder said: "That's probably the lab boys. I told them to come over here as soon as they could finish up at the cathedral."

Mike checked his screen and when Cowder identified the men at the door, Mike let them in.

The short, chubby man in the lead, who was introduced as Perkins, spoke to Sergeant Cowder first. "We checked one of those rockets. Almost a professional job. TNT war head, surrounded by a jacket filled with liquid HCN and a phosphate inhibitor to prevent polymerization. Nasty things." He swung around to Mike. "You're lucky you weren't in the room, or you'd just be

43

part of the wreckage, Mr. Gabriel."

"I know," said Mike the Angel. "Well, the room's all yours. It probably won't tell you much."

"Probably not," said Perkins, "but we'll see. Come on, boys."

Mike the Angel tapped Cowder on the shoulder. "I'd like to talk to you for a minute."

Cowder nodded, and Mike led the way back into his private office. He opened his desk drawer and took out the little pack that housed the workings of the vibroblade shield.

"That accident you were talking about, Sergeant— the one that made those vibroblades blow, remember? I got to thinking that maybe this could have caused it. I think that with a little more power, it might even vaporize a high-speed bullet. But I'd advise you to wear asbestos clothing."

Cowder took the thing and looked at it. "Thanks, Mr. Gabriel," he said honestly. "Maybe the kids will go on to using something else if vibroblades don't work, but I think I'd prefer a rocket in the head to being carved by a vibro."

"To be honest," Mike said, "I think the vibro is just a fad among the JD's now, anyway. You know—if you're one of the real biggies, you carry a vibro. A year from now, it might be shock guns, but right now you're chicken if you carry anything but a vibroblade."

Cowder dropped the shield generator into his coat pocket. "Thanks again, Mr. Gabriel. We'll do you a favor sometime."

6

The firm of M. R. GABRIEL, POWER DESIGN was not a
giant corporation, but it did pretty well for a one-man
show. The outer office was a gauntlet that Mike the Angel
had to run when he came in the next morning after
having spent the night at a hotel. There was a mixed and
ragged chorus of "Good morning, Mr. Gabriel" as he
passed through. Mike gave the nod to each of them and
was stopped four times for small details before he
finally made his way to his own office.

His secretary was waiting for him. She was short,
bony, and plain of face. She had a figure like an ironing
board and the soul of a Ramsden calculator. Mike the
Angel liked her that way; it avoided complications.

"Good morning, Mr. Gabriel," she said. "What the
hell happened here?" She waved at the warped door and
the ribbons of electrostatic tape that still lay in curls on
the floor.

Mike told her, and she listened to his recitation
without any change of expression. "I'm very glad you
weren't hurt," she said when he had finished. "What

are you going to do about the apartment?"

Mike opened the heavy door and looked at the wreckage inside. Through the gaping hole of the shattered window, he could see the towering spires of the two-hundred-year-old Cathedral of St. John the Divine. "Get Larry Beasley on the phone, Helen. I've forgotten his number, but you'll find him listed under 'Interior Decorators.' He has the original plans and designs on file. Tell him to get them out; I want this place fixed up just like it was."

"But what if someone else . . ." She gestured toward the broken window and the cathedral spires beyond.

"When you're through talking to Beasley," Mike went on, "see if you can get Bishop Brennan on the phone and switch him to my desk."

"Yes, sir," she said.

Within two hours workmen were busily cleaning up the wreckage in Mike the Angel's apartment, and the round, plump figure of Larry Beasley was walking around pompously while his artistic but businesslike brain made estimates. Mike had also reached an agreement with the bishop whereby special vaultlike doors would be fitted into the stairwells leading up to the towers at Mike's expense. They were to have facings of bronze so that they could be decorated to blend with the Gothic decor of the church, but the bronze would be backed by heavy steel. Nobody would blow *those* down in a hurry.

Since the wrecked living room was a flurry of activity and his office had become a thoroughfare, Mike the Angel retired to his bedroom to think. He took with him the microcryotron stack he had picked up at Old Harry's the night before.

"For something that doesn't look like much," he said aloud to the stack, "you have caused me a hell of a lot of trouble."

Old Harry, he knew, wouldn't be caught dead selling the things. In the first place, it was strictly illegal to deal in the components of robotic brains. In the second place, they were so difficult to get, even on the black market, that the few that came into Old Harry's hands went into the defenses of his own shop. Mike the Angel had only wanted to borrow one to take a good look at it. He had read up on all the literature about microcryotrons, but he'd never actually seen one before.

He had reason to be curious about microcryotrons. There was something definitely screwy going on in Antarctica.

Nearly two years before, the UN Government, in the person of Minister Wallingford himself, had asked Mike's firm—which meant Mike the Angel himself—to design the power drive and the thrust converters for a spaceship. On the face of it, there was nothing at all unusual in that. Such jobs were routine for M. R. Gabriel.

But when the specifications arrived, Mike the Angel had begun to wonder what the devil was going on. The spaceship *William Branchell* was to be built on the surface of Earth—and yet it was to be a much larger ship than any that had ever before been built on the ground. Usually, an interstellar vessel that large was built in orbit around the Earth, where the designers didn't have to worry about gravitational pull. Such a ship never landed, any more than an ocean liner was ever beached—not on purpose, anyway. The passengers and cargo were taken up by smaller vessels and brought down the same way when the liner arrived at her destination.

Aside from the tremendous energy required to lift such a vessel free of a planet's surface, there was also the magnetic field of the planet to consider. The drive tubes tended to wander and become erratic if they were forced to cut through the magnetic field of a planet.

Therefore, Question One: Why wasn't the *Branchell* being built in space?

Part of the answer, Mike knew, lay in the specifications for the construction of Cargo Hold One. For one thing, it was huge. For another, it was heavily insulated. For a third, it was built like a tank for holding liquids. All very well and good; possibly someone wanted to carry a cargo of cold lemonade or iced tea. That would be pretty stupid, maybe, but it wouldn't be mysterious.

The mystery lay in the fact that Cargo Hold One had *already been built*. The *Branchell* was to be built *around* it! And that didn't exactly jibe with Mike the Angel's ideas of the proper way to build a spaceship. It was not quite the same as building a seagoing vessel around an oil tank in the middle of Texas, but it was close enough to bother Mike the Angel.

Therefore, Question Two: Why was the *Branchell* being built around Cargo Hold One?

Which led to Question Three: What was *in* Cargo Hold One?

For the answer to that question, he had one very good hint. The density of the contents of Cargo Hold One was listed in the specs as being one-point-seven-two-six grams per cubic centimeter. And that, Mike happened to know, was the density of a cryotronic brain, which is 90 per cent liquid helium and 10 per cent tantalum and niobium, by volume.

He looked at the microcryotron stack in his hand. It was a one-hundred-kilounit stack. The possible connections within it were factorial one hundred thousand. All it needed was to be immersed in its bath of liquid helium to make the metals superconducting, and it would be ready to go to work.

A friend of his who worked for Computer Corporation of Earth had built a robot once, using just such a stack. The robot was designed to play poker. He had fed in all the rules of play and added all the data from Oesterveldt's *On Poker*. It took Mike the Angel exactly one hour to figure out how to beat it.

As long as Mike played rationally, the machine had a slight edge, since it had a perfect memory and could compute faster than Mike could. But it would not, could not learn how to bluff. As soon as Mike started bluffing, the robot went into a tizzy.

It wouldn't have been so bad if the robot had known nothing whatever about bluffing. That would have made it easy for Mike. All he'd have had to do was keep on feeding in chips until the robot folded.

But the robit *did* know about bluffing. The trouble is that bluffing is essentially illogical, and the robot had no rules whatsoever to go by to judge whether Mike was bluffing or not. It finally decided to make its decisions by chance, judging by Mike's past performance at bluffing. When it did, Mike quit bluffing and cleaned it out fast.

That caused such utter confusion in the random circuits that Mike's friend had had to spend a week cleaning up the robot's little mind.

But what would be the purpose of building a brain as gigantic as the one in Cargo Hold One? And why build a spaceship around it?

Like a pig roasting on an automatic spit, the problem kept turning over and over in Mike's mind. And, like the roasting pig, the time eventually came when it was done.

Once it is set in operation, a properly operating robot brain can neither be shut off nor dismantled. Not, that is, unless you want to lose all of the data and processes you've fed into it.

Now, suppose the Computer Corporation of Earth had built a giant-sized brain. (Never mind *why*—just suppose.) And suppose they wanted to take it off Earth, but didn't want to lose all the data that had been pumped into it. (Again, never mind *why*—just suppose.)

Very well, then. *If* such a brain had been built, and *if* it was necessary to take it off Earth, and *if* the data in it was so precious that the brain could not be shut off or dismantled, *then* the thing to do would be to build a ship around it.

Oh *yeah*?

Mike the Angel stared at the microcryotron stack and asked:

"Now, tell me, pal, just why would anyone want a brain that big? And what is so blasted important about it?"

The stack said not a word.

The phone chimed. Mike the Angel thumbed the switch, and his secretary's face appeared on the screen. "Minister Wallingford is on the line, Mr. Gabriel."

"Put him on," said Mike the Angel.

Basil Wallingford's ruddy face came on. "I see you're still alive," he said. "What in the bloody blazes happened last night?"

50

Mike sighed and told him. "In other words," he ended up, "just the usual sort of JD stuff we have to put up with these days. Nothing new, and nothing to worry about."

"You almost got killed," Wallingford pointed out.

"A miss is as good as a mile," Mike said with cheerful inanity. "Thanks to your phone call, I was as safe as if I'd been in my own home," he added with utter illogic.

"You can afford to laugh," Wallingford said grimly. "I can't. I've already lost one man."

Mike's grin vanished. "What do you mean? Who?"

"Oh, nobody's killed," Wallingford said quickly. "I didn't mean that. But Jack Wong turned his car over yesterday at a hundred and seventy miles an hour, and he's laid up with a fractured leg and a badly dislocated arm."

"Too bad," said Mike. "One of these days that fool will kill himself racing." He knew Wong and liked him. They had served together in the Space Service when Mike was on active duty.

"I hope not," Wallingford said. "Anyway—the matter I called on last night. Can you get those specs for me?"

"Sure, Wally. Hold on." He punched the hold button and rang for his secretary as Wallingford's face vanished. When the girl's face came on, he said: "Helen, get me the cargo specs on the *William Branchell*—Section Twelve, pages 66 to 74."

The discussion, after Helen had brought the papers, lasted less than five minutes. It was merely a matter of straightening out some cost estimates—but since it had to do with the *Branchell*, and specifically with Hold

51

Number One, Mike decided he'd ask a question.

"Wally, tell me—what in the hell is going on down there at Chilblains Base?"

"They're building a spaceship," said Wallingford in a flat voice.

It was Wallingford's way of saying he wasn't going to answer any questions, but Mike the Angel ignored the hint. "I'd sort of gathered that," he said dryly. "But what I want to know is: Why is it being built around a cryotronic brain, the like of which I have never heard before?"

Basil Wallingford's eyes widened, and he just stared for a full two seconds. "And just how did you come across that information, Golden Wings?" he finally asked.

"It's right here in the specs," said Mike the Angel, tapping the sheaf of papers.

"Ridiculous." Wallingford's voice seemed toneless.

Mike decided he was in too deep now to back out. "It certainly is, Wally. It couldn't be hidden. To compute the thrust stresses, I had to know the density of the contents of Cargo Hold One. And here it is: 1.726 gm/cm^8. Nothing else that I know of has that exact density."

Wallingford pursed his lips. "Dear me," he said after a moment. "I keep forgetting you're too bright for your own good." Then a slow smile spread over his face. "Would you *really* like to know?"

"I wouldn't have asked otherwise," Mike said.

"Fine. Because you're just the man we need."

Mike the Angel could almost feel the knife blade sliding between his ribs, and he had the uncomfortable feeling that the person who had stabbed him in the back was himself. "What's that supposed to mean, Wally?"

"You are, I believe, an officer in the Space Service Reserve," said Basil Wallingford in a smooth, too oily voice. "Since the Engineering Officer of the *Branchell*, Jack Wong, is laid up in a hospital, I'm going to call you to active duty to replace him."

Mike the Angel felt that ghostly knife twist—hard.

"That's silly," he said. "I haven't been a ship's officer for five years."

"You're the man who designed the power plant," Wallingford said sweetly. "If you don't know how to run her, nobody does."

"My time per hour is worth a great deal," Mike pointed out.

"The rate of pay for a Space Service officer," Basil Wallingford said pleasantly, "is fixed by law."

"I can fight being called back to duty—and I'll win," said Mike. He didn't know how long he could play this game, but it was fun.

"True," said Wallingford. "You can. I admit it. But you've been wondering what the hell that ship is being built for. You'd give your left arm to find out. I know you, Golden Wings, and I know how that mind of yours works. And I tell you this: Unless you take this job, you'll *never* find out why the *Branchell* was built." He leaned forward, and his face loomed large in the screen. "And I mean absolutely *never*."

For several seconds Mike the Angel said nothing. His classically handsome face was like that of some Grecian god contemplating the Universe, or an archangel contemplating Eternity. Then he gave Basil Wallingford the benefit of his full, radiant smile.

"I capitulate," he said.

Wallingford refused to look impressed. "Damn right you do," he said—and cut the circuit.

7

Two days later Mike the Angel was sitting at his desk making certain that M. R. GABRIEL, POWER DESIGN would function smoothly while he was gone. Serge Paulvitch, his chief designer, could handle almost everything.

Paulvitch had once said, "Mike, the hell of working for a first-class genius is that a second-class genius doesn't have a chance."

"You could start your own firm," Mike had said levelly. "I'll back you, Serge; you know that."

Serge Paulvitch had looked astonished. "Me? You think I'm crazy? Right now, I'm a second-class genius working for a first-class outfit. You think I want to be a second-class genius working for a second-class outfit? Not on your life!"

Serge Paulvitch could easily handle the firm for a few weeks.

Helen's face came on the phone. "There's a Captain Sir Henry Quill on the phone, Mr. Gabriel. Do you wish to speak to him?"

"Black Bart?" said Mike. "I wonder what he wants."

"Bart?" She looked puzzled. "He said his name was Henry."

Mike grinned. "He always signs his name: *Captain Sir Henry Quill, Bart.* And since he's the toughest old martinet this side of the Pleiades, the 'Black' part just comes naturally. I served under him seven years ago. Put him on."

In half a second the grim face of Captain Quill was on the screen.

He was as bald as an egg. What little hair he did have left was meticulously shaved off every morning. He more than made up for his lack of cranial growth, however, by his great, shaggy, bristly brows, black as jet and firmly anchored to jutting supraorbital ridges. Any other man would have been proud to wear them as mustaches.

"What can I do for you, Captain?" Mike asked, using the proper tone of voice prescribed for the genial businessman.

"You can go out and buy yourself a new uniform," Quill growled. "Your old one isn't regulation any more."

Well, not exactly growled. If he'd had the voice for it, it would have been a growl, but the closest he could come to a growl was an Irish tenor rumble with undertones of gravel. He stood five-eight, and his red and gold Space Service uniform gleamed with spit-and-polish luster. With his cap off, his bald head looked as though it, too, had been polished.

Mike looked at him thoughtfully. "I see. So you're commanding the mystery tub, eh?" he said at last.

"That's right," said the captain. "And don't go asking me a bunch of blasted questions. I've got no more idea of what the bloody thing's about than you—maybe not as much. I understand you designed her power plant . . . ?"

He let it hang. If not exactly a leading question, it was certainly a hinting statement.

Mike shook his head. "I don't know anything, Captain. Honestly I don't."

If Space Service regulations had allowed it, Captain Sir Henry Quill, Bart., would have worn a walrus mustache. And if he'd had such a mustache, he would have whuffled it then. As it was, he just blew out air, and nothing whuffled.

"You and I are the only ones in the dark, then," he said. "The rest of the crew is being picked from Chilblains Base. Pete Jeffers is First Officer, in case you're wondering."

"Oh great," Mike the Angel said with a moan. "That means we'll be going in cold on an untried ship."

Like Birnam Wood advancing on Dunsinane, Quill's eyebrows moved upward. "Don't you trust your own designing?"

"As much as you do," said Mike the Angel. "Probably more."

Quill nodded. "We'll have to make the best of it. We'll muddle through somehow. Are you all ready to go?"

"No," Mike admitted, "but I don't see that I can do a damn thing about that."

"Nor do I," said Captain Quill. "Be at Chilblains Base in twenty-four hours. Arrangements will be made at the Long Island Base for your transportation to

Antarctica. And"—he paused and his scowl became deeper—"you'd best get used to calling me 'sir' again."

"Yessir, Sir Henry, sir."

"*Thank* you, Mister Gabriel," snapped Quill, cutting the circuit.

"Selah," said Mike the Angel.

Chilblains Base, Antarctica, was directly over the South Magnetic Pole—at least, as closely as that often elusive spot could be pinpointed for any length of time. It is cheaper in the long run if an interstellar vessel moves parallel with, not perpendicular to, the magnetic "lines of force" of a planet's gravitational field. Taking off "across the grain" *can* be done, but the power consumption is much greater. Taking off "with the grain" is expensive enough.

An ion rocket doesn't much care where it lifts or sets down, since its method of propulsion isn't trying to work against the fabric of space itself. For that reason, an interstellar vessel is normally built in space and stays there, using ion rockets for loading and unloading its passengers. It's cheaper by far.

The Computer Corporation of Earth had also been thinking of expenses when it built its Number One Research Station near Chilblains Base, although the corporation was not aware at the time just how much money it was eventually going to save them.

The original reason had simply been lower power costs. A cryotron unit has to be immersed at all times in a bath of liquid helium at a temperature of four-point-two degrees absolute. It is obviously much easier—and much cheaper—to keep several thousand gallons of helium at that temperature if the surrounding temperature is at two hundred thirty-three absolute than if it is up around two hundred ninety or three hundred. That may not seem like much percentagewise, but it comes out to a substantial saving in the long run.

But, power consumption or no, when C.C. of E. found that Snookums either had to be moved or destroyed, it was mightily pleased that it had built Prime Station near Chilblains Base. Since a great deal of expense also, of necessity, devolved upon Earth Government, the government was, to say it modestly, equally pleased. There was enough expense as it was.

The scenery at Chilblains Base—so named by a wise-acre American navy man back in the twentieth century—was nothing to brag about. Thousands of square miles of powdered ice that has had nothing to do but blow around for twenty million years is not at all inspiring after the first few minutes unless one is obsessed by the morbid beauty of cold death.

Mike the Angel was not so obsessed. To him, the area surrounding Chilblains Base was just so much white hell, and his analysis was perfectly correct. Mike wished that it had been January, midsummer in the Antarctic, so there would have been at least a little dim sunshine. Mike the Angel did not particularly relish having to visit the South Pole in midwinter.

The rocket that had lifted Mike the Angel from Long Island Base settled itself into the snow-covered landing stage of Chilblains Base, dissipating the crystalline whiteness into steam as it did so. The steam, blown away by the chill winds, moved all of thirty yards before it became ice again.

Mike the Angel was not in the best of moods. Having to dump all of his business into Serge Paulvitch's hands on twenty-four hours' notice was irritating. He knew

Paulvitch could handle the job, but it wasn't fair to him to make him take over so suddenly.

In addition, Mike did not like the way the whole *Branchell* business was being handled. It seemed slipshod and hurried, and, worse, it was entirely too mysterious and melodramatic.

"Of all the times to have to come to Antarctica," he grumped as the door of the rocket opened, "why did I have to get July?"

The pilot, a young man in his early twenties, said smugly: "July is bad, but January isn't good—just not so worse."

Mike the Angel glowered. "Sonny, I was a cadet here when you were learning arithmetic. It hasn't changed since, summer or winter."

"Sorry, sir," said the pilot stiffly.

"So am I," said Mike the Angel cryptically. "Thanks for the ride."

He pushed open the outer door, pulled his electroparka closer around him, and stalked off across the walk, through the lashing of the sleety wind.

He didn't have far to walk—a hundred yards or so—but it was a good thing that the walk was protected and well within the boundary of Chilblains Base instead of being out on the Wastelands. Here there were lights, and the Hotbed equipment of the walk warmed the swirling ice particles into a sleety rain. On the Wastelands, the utter blackness and the wind-driven snow would have swallowed him permanently within ten paces.

He stepped across a curtain of hot air that blew up from a narrow slit in the deck and found himself in the main foyer of Chilblains Base.

The entrance looked like the entrance to a theater—a big metal and plastic opening, like a huge room open on one side, with only that sheet of hot air to protect it from the storm raging outside. The lights and the small doors leading into the building added to the impression that this was a theater, not a military base.

But the man who was standing near one of the doors was not by a long shot dressed as an usher. He wore a sergeant's stripes on his regulation Space Service parka, which muffled him to the nose, and he came over to Mike the Angel and said: "Commander Gabriel?"

Mike the Angel nodded as he shook icy drops from his gloved hands, then fished in his belt pocket for his newly printed ID card.

He handed it to the sergeant, who looked it over, peered at Mike's face, and saluted. As Mike returned the salute the sergeant said: "Okay, sir; you can go on in. The security office is past the double door, first corridor on your right."

Mike the Angel tried his best not to look surprised. "*Security* office? Is there a war on or something? What does Chilblains need with a security office?"

The sergeant shrugged. "Don't ask me, Commander; I just slave away here. Maybe Lieutenant Nariaki knows something, but I sure don't."

"Thanks, Sergeant."

Mike the Angel went inside, through two insulated and tightly weather-stripped doors, one right after another, like the air lock on a spaceship. Once inside the warmth of the corridor, he unzipped his electroparka, shut off the power, and pushed back the hood with its fogproof faceplate.

Down the hall, Mike could see an office marked

security officer in small letters without capitals. He walked toward it. There was another guard at the door who had to see Mike's ID card before Mike was allowed in.

Lieutenant Tokugawa Nariaki was an average-sized, sleepy-looking individual with a balding crew cut and a morose expression.

He looked up from his desk as Mike came in, and a hopeful smile tried to spread itself across his face. "If you are Commander Gabriel," he said softly, "watch yourself. I may suddenly kiss you out of sheer relief."

'Restrain yourself, then," said Mike the Angel, "because I'm Gabriel."

Nariaki's smile became genuine. "So! Good! The phone has been screaming at me every half hour for the past five hours. Captain Sir Henry Quill wants you."

"He would," Mike said. "How do I get to him?"

"You don't just yet," said Nariaki, raising a long, bony, tapering hand. "There are a few formalities which our guests have to go through."

"Such as?"

"Such as fingerprint and retinal patterns," said Lieutenant Nariaki.

Mike cast his eyes to Heaven in silent appeal, then looked back at the lieutenant. "Lieutenant, *what* is going on here? There hasn't been a security officer in the Space Service for thirty years or more. What am I suspected of? Spying for the corrupt and evil alien beings of Diomega Orionis IX?"

Nariaki's oriental face became morose again. "For all I know, you are. Who knows what's going on around here?" He got up from behind his desk and led Mike the Angel over to the fingerprinting machine. "Put your hands in here, Commander . . . that's it."

He pushed a button, and, while the machine hummed, he said: "Mine is an antiquated position, I'll admit. I don't like it any more than you do. Next thing, they'll put me to work polishing chain-mail armor or make me commander of a company of musketeers. Or maybe they'll send me to the 18th Outer Mongolian Yak Artillery."

Mike looked at him with narrowed eyes. "Lieutenant, do you actually mean that you really don't know what's going on here, or are you just dummying up?"

Nariaki looked at Mike, and for the first time, his face took on the traditional blank, emotionless look of the "placid Orient." He paused for long seconds, then said:

"Some of both, Commander. But don't let it worry you. I assure you that within the next hour you'll know more about Project Brainchild than I've been able to find out in two years . . . Now put your face in here and keep your eyes open. When you can see the target spot, focus on it and tell me."

Mike the Angel put his face in the rest for the retinal photos. The soft foam rubber adjusted around his face, and he was looking into blackness. He focused his eyes on the dim target circle and waited for his eyes to grow accustomed to the darkness.

The Security Officer's voice continued. "All I do is make sure that no unauthorized person comes into Chilblains Base. Other than that, I have nothing but personal guesses and little trickles of confusing information, neither of which am I at liberty to discuss."

Mike's irises had dilated to the point that he could see the dim dot in the center of the target circle, glowing like a dimly visible star. "Shoot," he said.

There was a dazzling glare of light. Mike pulled his face out of the padded opening and blinked away the colored after-images.

Lieutenant Nariaki was comparing the fresh fingerprints with the set he had had on file. "Well," he said. "you have Commander Gabriel's hands, anyway. If you have his eyes, I'll have to concede that the rest of the body belongs to him, too."

"How about my soul?" Mike asked dryly.

"Not my province, Commander," Nariaki said as he pulled the retinal photos out of the machine. "Maybe one of the chaplains would know."

"If this sort of thing is going on all over Chilblains," said Mike the Angel, "I imagine the Office of Chaplains is doing a booming business in TS cards."

The lieutenant put the retinal photos in the comparator, took a good look, and nodded. "You're you," he said. "Give me your ID card."

Mike handed it over, and Nariaki fed it through a printer which stamped a complex seal in the upper left-hand corner of the card. The lieutenant signed his name across the seal and handed the card back to Mike.

"That's it," he said. "You can—"

He was interrupted by the chiming of the phone.

"Just a second, Commander," he said as he thumbed the phone switch.

Mike was out of range of the TV pickup, and he couldn't see the face on the screen, but the voice was so easy to recognize that he didn't need to see the man.

"Hasn't that triply bedamned rocket landed yet, Lieutenant? Where is Commander Gabriel?"

Mike knew that Black Bart had already checked on

the landing of the latest rocket; the question was rhetorical.

Mike grinned. "Tell the old tyrant," he said firmly, "that I'll be along as soon as the Security Officer is through with me."

Nariaki's expression didn't change. "You're through now, Commander, and—"

"Tell that imitation Apollo to hop it over here fast!" said Quill sharply. "I'll give him a lesson in tyranny."

There was a click as the intercom shut off.

Nariaki looked at Mike the Angel and shook his head slowly. "Either you're working your way toward a courtmartial or else you know where Black Bart has the body buried."

"I should," said Mike cryptically. "I helped him bury it. How do I get to His Despotic Majesty's realm?"

Nariaki considered. "It'll take you five or six minutes. Take the tubeway to Stage Twelve. Go up the stairway to the surface and take the first corridor to the left. That'll take you to the loading dock for that stage. It's an open foyer like the one at the landing field, so you'll have to put your parka back on. Go down the stairs on the other side, and you'll be in Area K. One of the guards will tell you where to go from there. Of course, you could go by tube, but it would take longer because of the by-pass."

"Good enough. I'll take the short cut. See you. And thanks."

8

The underground tubeway shot Mike the Angel across five miles of track at high speed. Mike left the car at Stage Twelve and headed up the stairway and down the corridor to a heavy double door marked *freight loading*.

He put on his parka and went through the door. The foyer was empty, and, like the one at the rocket landing, protected from the Antarctic blast only by a curtain of hot air. Outside that curtain, the light seemed to lose itself in the darkness of the bleak, snow-filled Wastelands. Mike ignored the snowscape and headed across the empty foyer to the door marked *entrance*.

"With a small *e*," Mike muttered to himself. "I wonder if the sign painter ran out of full caps."

He was five feet from the door when he heard the yell.

"*Help!*"

That was all. Just the one word.

Mike the Angel came to a dead halt and spun around.

The foyer was a large room, about fifty by fifty feet in area and nearly twenty feet high. And it was quite obviously empty. On the open side, the sheet of hissing hot air was doing its best to shield the room from the sixty-below-zero blizzard outside. Opposite the air curtain was a huge sliding door, closed at the moment, which probably led to a freight elevator. There were only two other doors leading from the foyer, and both of them were closed. And Mike knew that no voice could come through those insulated doors.

"*Help!*"

Mike the Angel swung toward the air curtain. This time there was no doubt. Someone was out in that howling ice-cloud, screaming for help!

Mike saw the figure—dimly, fleetingly, obscured most of the time by the driving whiteness. Whoever it was looked as if he were buried to the waist in snow.

Mike made a quick estimate. It was dark out there, but he could see the figure; therefore he would be able to see the foyer lights. He wouldn't get lost. Snapping down the faceplate of his parka hood, he ran through the protective updraft of the air curtain and charged into the deadly chill of the Antarctic blizzard.

In spite of the electroparka he was wearing, the going was difficult. The snow tended to plaster itself against his faceplate, and the wind kept trying to take him off his feet. He wiped a gloved hand across the faceplate. Ahead, he could still see the figure waving its arms. Mike slogged on.

At sixty below, frozen H_2O isn't slushy, by any means; it isn't even slippery. It's more like fine sand than anything else. Mike the Angel figured he had about thirty feet to go, but after he'd taken eight steps, the arm-waving figure looked as far off as when he'd started.

Mike stopped and flipped up his faceplate. It felt as though someone had thrown a handful of razor blades into his face. He winced and yelled, "What's the trouble?" Then he snapped the plate back into position.

"I'm cold!" came the clear, contralto voice through the howling wind.

A *woman*! thought Mike. "I'm coming!" he bellowed, pushing on. Ten more steps.

He stopped again. He couldn't see anyone or anything.

He flipped up his faceplate. "Hey!"

No answer.

"Hey!" he called again.

And still there was no answer.

Around Mike the Angel, there was nothing but the swirling, blinding snow, the screaming, tearing wind, and the blackness of the Antarctic night.

There was something damned odd going on here. Carefully putting the toe of his foot to the rear of the heel of his left, he executed a one-hundred-eighty-degree military about-face.

And breathed a sigh of relief.

He could still see the lights of the foyer. He had half suspected that someone was trying to trap him out here, and they might have turned off the lights.

He swiveled his head around for one last look. He still couldn't see a sign of anyone. There was nothing he could do but head back and report the incident. He started slogging back through the gritty snow.

He stepped through the hot-air curtain and flipped up his faceplate.

"Why did you go out in the blizzard?" said a clear, contralto voice directly behind him.

Mike swung around angrily. "Look, lady, I—"

He stopped.

The lady was no lady.

A few feet away stood a machine. Vaguely humanoid in shape from the waist up, it was built more like a miniature military tank from the waist down. It had a pair of black sockets in its head, which Mike took to be TV cameras of some kind. It had grillwork on either side of its head, which probably covered microphones, and another grillwork where the mouth should be. There was no nose.

"What the hell?" asked Mike the Angel of no one in particular.

"I'm Snookums," said the robot.

"Sure you are," said Mike the Angel, backing uneasily toward the door. "You're Snookums. I couldn't fail not to disagree with you less."

Mike the Angel didn't particularly like being frightened, but he had never found it a disabling emotion, so he could put up with it if he had to. But, given his choice, he would have much preferred to be afraid of something a little less unpredictable, something he knew a little more about. Something comfortable, like, say, a Bengal tiger or a Kodiak bear.

"But I really *am* Snookums," reiterated the clear voice.

Mike's brain was functioning in high gear with overdrive added and the accelerator floor-boarded. He'd been lured out onto the Wastelands by this machine—it most definitely could be dangerous.

The robot was obviously a remote-control device. The arms and hands were of the waldo type used to handle radioactive materials in a hot lab—four jointed fingers and an opposed thumb, metal duplicates of the human hand.

But who was on the other end? Who was driving the machine? Who was saying those inane things over the speaker that served the robot as a mouth? It was certainly a woman's voice.

Mike was still moving backward, toward the door. The machine that called itself Snookums wasn't moving toward him, which was some consolation, but not much. The thing could obviously move faster on those treads than Mike could on his feet. Especially since Mike was moving backward.

"Would you mind explaining what this is all about, miss?" asked Mike the Angel. He didn't expect an explanation; he was stalling for time.

"I am not a 'miss,'" said the robot. "I am Snookums."

"Whatever you are, then," said Mike, "would you mind explaining?"

"No," said Snookums, "I wouldn't mind."

Mike's fingers, groping behind him, touched the door handle. But before he could grasp it, it turned, and the door opened behind him. It hit him full in the back, and he stumbled forward a couple of steps before regaining his balance.

A clear contralto voice said: "Oh! I'm so sorry!"

It was the same voice as the robot's!

Mike the Angel swung around to face the second robot.

This time it was a lady.

"I'm sorry," she repeated. She was all wrapped up in an electroparka, but there was no mistaking the fact that she was both human and feminine. She came on through the door and looked at the robot. "Snookums! What are you doing here?"

"I was trying an experiment, Leda," said Snookums. "This man was just asking me about it. I just wanted to see if he would come if I called 'help.' He did, and I want to know *why* he did."

The girl flashed a look at Mike. "Would you please tell Snookums why you went out there? Please—don't be angry or anything—just tell him."

Mike was beginning to get the picture. "I went because I thought I heard a human being calling for help—and it sounded suspiciously like a woman."

"Oh," said Snookums, sounding a little downhearted—if a robot can be said to have a heart. "The reaction was based, then, upon a misconception. That makes the data invalid. I'll have to try again."

"That won't be necessary, Snookums," the girl said firmly. "This man went out there because he thought a human life was in danger. He would not have done it if he had known it was you, because he would have known that you were not in any danger. You can stand much lower temperatures than a human being can, you know." She turned to Mike. "Am I correct in saying that you wouldn't have gone out there if you'd known Snookums was a robot?"

"Absolutely correct," said Mike the Angel fervently.

She looked back at Snookums. "Don't try that experiment again. It is dangerous for a human to go out there, even with an electroparka. You might run the risk of endangering human life."

"Oh dear!" said Snookums. "I'm sorry, Leda!" There was real anxiety in the voice.

"That's all right, honey," the girl said hurriedly. "This man isn't hurt, so don't get upset. Come along

72

now, and we'll go back to the lab. You shouldn't come out like this without permission.''

Mike had noticed that the girl had kept one hand on her belt all the time she was talking—and that her thumb was holding down a small button on a case attached to the belt.

He had been wondering why, but he didn't have to wonder long.

The door behind him opened again, and four men came out, obviously in a devil of a hurry. Each one of them was wearing a brassard labeled SECURITY POLICE.

At least, thought Mike the Angel as he turned to look them over, *the brassards aren't in all lower-case italics*.

One of them jerked a thumb at Mike. "This the guy, Miss Crannon?"

The girl nodded. "That's him. He saw Snookums. Take care of him." She looked again at Mike. "I'm terribly sorry, really I am. But there's no help for it." Then, without another word, she opened the door and went back inside, and the robot rolled in after her.

As the door closed behind her, the SP man nearest Mike, a tough-looking bozo wearing an ensign's insignia, said: "Let's see your identification."

Mike realized that his own parka had no insignia of rank on it, but he didn't like the SP man's tone.

"Come on!" snapped the ensign. "Who are you?"

Mike the Angel pulled out his ID card and handed it to the security cop. "It tells right there who I am," he said. "That is, if you can read."

The man glared and jerked the card out of Mike's hand, but when he saw the emblem that Lieutenant Nariaki had stamped on it, his eyes widened. He looked up at Mike. "I'm sorry, sir; I didn't mean—"

"That tears it," interrupted Mike. "That absolutely

73

tears it. In the past three minutes I have been apologized to by a woman, a robot, and a cop. The next thing, a penguin will walk in here, tip his top hat, and abase himself while he mutters obsequiously in penguinese. Just what the devil is going on around this place?"

The four SP men were trying hard not to fidget.

"Just security precautions, sir," said the ensign uncomfortably. "Nobody but those connected with Project Brainchild are supposed to know about Snookums. If anyone else finds out, we're supposed to take them into protective custody."

"I'll bet you're widely loved for that," said Mike. "I suppose the gadget at Miss What's-her-name's belt was an alarm to warn you of impending disaster?"

"Miss Crannon . . . Yes, sir. Everybody on the project carries those around. Also, Miss Crannon carries a detector for following Snookums around. She's sort of his keeper, you know."

"No," said Mike the Angel, "I do not know. But I intend to find out. I'm looking for Captain Quill; where is he?"

The four men looked at each other, then looked back at Mike.

"I don't know, Commander," said the ensign. "I understand that several new men have come in today, but I don't know all of them. You'd better talk to Dr. Fitzhugh."

"Such are the beauties of security," said Mike the Angel. "Where can I find this Dr. Fitzhugh?"

The security man looked at his wrist watch. "He's down in the cafeteria now, sir. It's coffee time, and Doc Fitzhugh is as regular as a satellite orbit."

"I'm glad you didn't say 'clockwork,' " Mike told

74

him. "I've had enough dealings with machines today. Where is this coffee haven?"

The ensign gave directions for reaching the cafeteria, and Mike pushed open the door marked *entrance*. He had to pass through another inner door guarded by another pair of SP men who checked his ID card again, then he had to ramble through hallways that went off at queer angles to each other, but he finally found the cafeteria.

He nabbed the first passer-by and asked him to point out Dr. Fitzhugh. The passer-by was obliging; he indicated a smallish, elderly man who was sitting by himself at one of the tables.

Mike made his way through the tray-carrying hordes that were milling about, and finally ended up at the table where the smallish man was sitting.

"Dr. Fitzhugh?" Mike offered his hand. "I'm Commander Gabriel. Minister Wallingford appointed me Engineering Officer of the *Branchell*."

Dr. Fitzhugh shook Mike's hand with apparent pleasure. "Oh yes. Sit down, Commander. What can I do for you?"

Mike had already peeled off his electroparka. He hung it over the back of a chair and said: "Mind if I grab a cup of coffee, Doctor? I've just come from topside, and I think the cold has made its way clean to my bones." He paused. "Would you like another cup?"

Dr. Fitzhugh looked at his watch. "I have time for one more, thanks."

By the time Mike had returned with the cups, he had recalled where he had heard the name Fitzhugh before.

"It just occurred to me," he said as he sat down.

"You must be Dr. *Morris* Fitzhugh."

Fitzhugh nodded. "That's right." He wore a perpetually worried look, which made his face look more wrinkled than his fifty years of age would normally have accounted for. Mike was privately of the opinion that if Fitzhugh ever really *tried* to look worried, his ears would meet over the bridge of his long nose.

"I've read a couple of your articles in the *Journal*," Mike explained, "but I didn't connect the name until I saw you. I recognized you from your picture."

Fitzhugh smiled, which merely served to wrinkle his face even more.

Mike the Angel spent the next several minutes feeling the man out, then he went on to explain what had happened with Snookums out in the foyer, which launched Dr. Fitzhugh into an explanation.

"He didn't want help, of course; he was merely conducting an experiment. There are many areas of knowledge in which he is as naïve as a child."

Mike nodded. "It figures. At first I thought he was just a remote-control tool, but I finally saw that he was a real, honest-to-goodness robot. Who gave him the idea to make such an experiment as that?"

"No one at all," said Dr. Fitzhugh. "He's built to make up his own experiments."

Mike the Angel's classic face regarded the wrinkled one of Dr. Fitzhugh. "His own experiments? But a robot—"

Fitzhugh held up a bony hand, gesturing for attention and silence. He got it from Mike.

"Snookums," he said, "is no ordinary robot, Commander."

Mike waited for more. When none came, he said: "So

I gather." He sipped at his black coffee. "That machine I saw is actually a remote-control tool, isn't it? Snookums' actual brain is in Cargo Hold One of the *William Branchell*."

"That's right." Dr. Fitzhugh began reaching into various pockets about his person. He extracted a tobacco pouch, a briar pipe, and a jet-flame lighter. Then he began speaking as he went through the pipe smoker's ritual of filling, tamping, and lighting.

"Snookums," he began, "is a self-activating, problem-seeking computer with input and output sensory and action mechanisms analogous to those of a human being." He pushed more tobacco into the bowl of his pipe with a bony forefinger. "He's as close to being a living creature as anything Man has yet devised."

"What about the synthecells they're making at Boston Med?" Mike asked, looking innocent.

Fitzhugh's contour-map face wrinkled up even more. "I should have said 'living *intelligence*,'" he corrected himself. "He's a true robot, in the old original sense of the word; an artificial entity that displays almost every function of a living, intelligent creature. And, at the same time, he has the accuracy and speed that is normal to a cryotron computer."

Mike the Angel said nothing while Fitzhugh fired up his lighter and directed the jet of flame into the bowl and puffed up great clouds of smoke which obscured his face.

While the roboticist puffed, Mike let his gaze wander idly over the other people in the cafeteria. He was wondering how much longer he could talk to Fitzhugh before Captain Quill began—

And then he saw the redhead.

There is never much point in describing a really beautiful girl. Each man has his own ideas of what it takes for a girl to be "pretty" or "fascinating" or "lovely" or almost any other adjective that can be applied to the noun "girl." But "beautiful" is a cultural concept, at least as far as females are concerned, and there is no point in describing a cultural concept. It's one of those things that everybody knows, and descriptions merely become repetitious and monotonous.

This particular example filled, in every respect, the definition of "beautiful" according to the culture of the white Americo-European subclass of the human race as of anno Domini 2087. The elements and proportions and symmetry fit almost perfectly into the ideal mold. It is only necessary to fill in some of the minor details which are allowed to vary without distorting the ideal.

She had red hair and blue eyes and was wearing a green zipsuit.

And she was coming toward the table where Mike and Dr. Fitzhugh were sitting.

". . . such a tremendous number of elements," Dr. Fitzhugh was saying, "that it was possible—and necessary—to introduce a certain randomness within the circuit choices themselves— Ah! Hello, Leda, my dear!"

Mike and Fitzhugh rose from their seats.

"Leda, this is Commander Gabriel, the Engineering Officer of the *Brainchild*," said Fitzhugh. "Commander, Miss Leda Crannon, our psychologist."

Mike had been allowing his eyes to wander over the girl, inspecting her ankles, her hair, and all vital points of interest between. But when he heard the name

"Crannon," his eyes snapped up to meet hers.

He hadn't recognized the girl without her parka and wouldn't have known her name if the SP ensign hadn't mentioned it. Obviously, she didn't recognize Mike at all, but there was a troubled look in her blue eyes.

She gave him a puzzled smile. "Haven't we met, Commander?"

Mike grinned. "Hey! That's supposed to be *my* line, isn't it?"

She flashed him a warm smile, then her eyes widened ever so slightly. "Your voice! You're the man on the foyer! The one . . ."

". . . the one whom you called copper on," finished Mike agreeably. "But please don't apologize; you've more than made up for it."

Her smile remained. She evidently liked what she saw. "How was I to know who you were?"

"It might have been written on my pocket handkerchief," said Mike the Angel, "but Space Service officers don't carry pocket handkerchiefs."

"What?" The puzzled look had returned.

"Ne' mind," said Mike. "Sit down, won't you?"

"Oh, I can't, thanks. I came to get Fitz; a meeting of the Research Board has been called, and afterward we have to give a lecture or something to the officers of the *Brainchild*."

"You mean the *Branchell*?"

Her smile became an impish grin. "You call it what you want. To us, it's the *Brainchild*."

Dr. Fitzhugh said: "Will you excuse us, Commander? We'll be seeing you at the briefing later."

Mike nodded. "I'd better get on my way, too. I'll see you."

79

But he stood there as Leda Crannon and Dr. Fitzhugh walked away. The girl looked just as divine retreating as she had advancing.

9

Captain Sir Henry (Black Bart) Quill was seated in an old-fashioned, formyl-covered, overstuffed chair, chewing angrily at the end of an unlighted cigar. His bald head gleamed like a pink billiard ball, almost matching the shining glory of his golden insignia against his scarlet tunic.

Mike the Angel had finally found his way through the maze of underground passageways to the door marked *wardroom* 9 and had pushed it open gingerly, halfway hoping that he wouldn't be seen coming in late but not really believing it would happen.

He was right. Black Bart was staring directly at the door when it slid open. Mike shrugged inwardly and stepped boldly into the room, flicking a glance over the faces of the other officers present.

"Well, well, well, Mister Gabriel," said Black Bart. The voice was oily, but the oil was oil of vitriol. "You not only come late, but you come incognito. Where is your uniform?"

81

There was a muffled snicker from one of the junior officers, but it wasn't muffled enough. Before Mike the Angel could answer, Captain Quill's head jerked around.

"That will do, Mister Vaneski!" he barked. "Boot ensigns don't snicker when their superiors—*and* their betters—are being reprimanded! I only use sarcasm on officers I respect. Until an officer earns my sarcasm, he gets nothing but blasting when he goofs off. Understand?"

The last word was addressed to the whole group.

Ensign Vaneski colored, and his youthful face became masklike. "Yes, sir. Sorry, sir."

Quill didn't even bother to answer; he looked back at Mike the Angel, who was still standing at attention. Quill's voice resumed its caustic saccharinity. "But don't let that go to your head, Mister Gabriel. I repeat: Where is your pretty red spaceman's suit?"

"If the Captain will recall," said Mike, "I had only twenty-four hours' notice. I couldn't get a new wardrobe in that time. It'll be in on the next rocket."

Captain Quill was silent for a moment, then he simply said, "Very well," thus dismissing the whole subject. He waved Mike the Angel to a seat. Mike sat.

"We'll dispense with the formal introductions," said Quill. "Commander Gabriel is our Engineering Officer. The rest of these boys all know each other, Commander; you and I are the only ones who don't come from Chilblains Base. You know Commander Jeffers, of course."

Mike nodded and grinned at Peter Jeffers, a lean, bony character who had a tendency to collapse into chairs as though he had come unhinged. Jeffers grinned and winked back.

"This is Lieutenant Commander von Liegnitz, Navigation Officer; Lieutenant Keku, Supply; Lieutenant Mellon, Medical Officer; and Ensign Vaneski, Maintenance. You can all shake hands with each other later; right now, let's get on with business." He frowned, overshadowing his eyes with those great, bushy brows. "What was I saying just before Commander Gabriel came in?"

Peter Jeffers shifted slightly in his seat. "You were sayin', suh, that this's the stupidest dam' assignment anybody evah got. Or words to that effect." Jeffers had been born in Georgia and had moved to the south of England at the age of ten. Consequently, his accent was far from standard.

"I think, Mister Jeffers," said Quill, "that I phrased it a bit more delicately, but that was the essence of it.

"The *Brainchild*, as she has been nicknamed, has been built at great expense for the purpose of making a single trip. We are to take her, and her cargo, to a destination known only to myself and von Liegnitz. We will be followed there by another Service ship, which will bring us back as passengers." He allowed himself a half-smile. "At least we'll get to loaf around on the way back."

The others grinned.

"The *Brainchild* will be left there and, presumably, dismantled."

He took the unlighted cigar out of his mouth, looked at it, and absently reached in his pocket for a lighter. The deeply tanned young man who had been introduced as Lieutenant Keku had just lighted a cigarette, so he proffered his own flame to the captain. Quill puffed his

83

cigar alight absently and went on.

"It isn't going to be easy. We won't have a chance to give the ship a shakedown cruise because once we take off we might as well keep going—which we will.

"You all know what the cargo is—Cargo Hold One contains the greatest single robotic brain ever built. Our job is to make sure it gets to our destination in perfect condition."

"Question, sir," said Mike the Angel.

Without moving his head, Captain Quill lifted one huge eyebrow and glanced in Mike's direction. "Yes?"

"Why didn't C.C. of E. build the brain on whatever planet we're going to in the first place?"

"We're supposed to be told that in the briefing over at the C.C. of E. labs in"—he glanced at his watch—"half an hour. But I think we can all get a little advance information. Most of you men have been around here long enough to have some idea of what's going on, but I understand that Mister Vaneski knows somewhat more about robotics than most of us. Do you have any light to shed on this, Mister Vaneski?"

Mike grinned to himself without letting it show on his face. The skipper was letting the boot ensign redeem himself after the *faux pas* he'd made.

Vaneski started to stand up, but Quill made a slight motion with his hand and the boy relaxed.

"It's only a guess, sir," he said, "but I think it's because the robot knows too much."

Quill and the others looked blank, but Mike narrowed his eyes imperceptibly. Vaneski was practically echoing Mike's own deductions.

"I mean—well, look, sir," Vaneski went on, a little flustered, "they started to build that thing ten years ago. Eight years ago they started teaching it. Evidently they didn't see any reason for building it off Earth then. What I mean is, something must've happened since then to make them decide to take it off Earth. If they've spent all this much money to get it away, that must mean that it's dangerous somehow."

"If that's the case," said Captain Quill, "why don't they just shut the thing off?"

"Well—" Vaneski spread his hands. "I think it's for the same reason. It knows too much, and they don't want to destroy that knowledge."

"Do you have any idea what that knowledge might be?" Mike the Angel asked.

"No, sir, I don't. But whatever it is, it's dangerous as hell."

The briefing for the officers and men of the *William Branchell*—the *Brainchild*— was held in a lecture room at the laboratories of the Computer Corporation of Earth's big Antarctic base.

Captain Quill spoke first, warning everyone that the project was secret and asking them to pay the strictest attention to what Dr. Morris Fitzhugh had to say.

Then Fitzhugh got up, his face ridged with nervousness. He assumed the air of a university professor, launching himself into his speech as though he were anxious to get through it in a given time without finishing too early.

"I'm sure you're all familiar with the situation," he said, as though apologizing to everyone for telling them something they already knew—the apology of the learned man who doesn't want anyone to think he's being overly proud of his learning.

"I think, however, we can all get a better picture if we

85

begin at the beginning and work our way up to the present time.

"The original problem was to build a computer that could learn by itself. An ordinary computer can be forcibly taught—that is, a technician can make changes in the circuits which will make the robot do something differently from the way it was done before, or even make it do something new.

"But what we wanted was a computer that could learn by itself, a computer that could make the appropriate changes in its own circuits without outside physical manipulation.

"It's really not as difficult as it sounds. You've all seen autoscribers, which can translate spoken words into printed symbols. An autoscriber is simply a machine which does what you tell it to—literally. Now, suppose a second computer is connected intimately with the first in such a manner that the second can, on order, change the circuits of the first. Then, all that is needed is . . ."

Mike looked around him while the roboticist went on. The men were looking pretty bored. They'd come to get a briefing on the reason for the trip, and all they were getting was a lecture on robotics.

Mike himself wasn't so much interested in the whys and wherefores of the trip; he was wondering why it was necessary to tell anyone—even the crew. Why not just pack Snookums up, take him to wherever he was going, and say nothing about it?

Why explain it to the crew?

"Thus," continued Fitzhugh, "it became necessary to incorporate into the brain a physical analogue of Lagerglocke's Principle: 'Learning is a result of an inelastic collision.'

"I won't give it to you symbolically, but the idea is simply that an organism learns *only* if it does *not* completely recover from the effects of an outside force imposed upon it. If it recovers completely, it's just as it was before. Consequently, it hasn't learned anything. *The organism must change.*"

He rubbed the bridge of his nose and looked out over the faces of the men before him. A faint smile came over his wrinkled features.

"Some of you, I know, are wondering why I am boring you with this long recital. Believe me, it's necessary. I want all of you to understand that the machine you will have to take care of is not just an ordinary computer. Every man here has had experience with machinery, from the very simplest to the relatively complex. You know that you have to be careful of the kind of information—the kind of external force—you give a machine.

"If you aim a spaceship at Mars, for instance, and tell it to go *through* the planet, it might try to obey, but you'd lose the machine in the process."

A ripple of laughter went through the men. They were a little more relaxed now, and Fitzhugh had regained their attention.

"And you must admit," Fitzhugh added, "a spaceship which was given that sort of information might be dangerous."

This time the laughter was even louder.

"Well, then," the roboticist continued, "if a mechanism is capable of learning, how do you keep it from becoming dangerous or destroying itself?

"That was the problem that faced us when we built

87

Snookums.

"So we decided to apply the famous Three Laws of Robotics propounded over a century ago by a brilliant American biochemist and philosopher.

"Here they are:

" *'One: A robot may not injure a human being, nor, through inaction, allow a human being to come to harm.'*

" *'Two: A robot must obey the orders given it by human beings except where such orders would conflict with the First Law.'*

" *'Three: A robot must protect its own existence as long as such protection does not conflict with the First or Second Law.'* "

Fitzhugh paused to let his words sink in, then: "Those are the ideal laws, of course. Even their propounder pointed out that they would be extremely difficult to put into practice. A robot is a logical machine, but it becomes somewhat of a problem even to define a human being. Is a five-year-old competent to give orders to a robot?

"If you define him as a human being, then he can give orders that might wreck an expensive machine. On the other hand, if you don't define the five-year-old as human, then the robot is under no compulsion to refrain from harming the child."

He began delving into his pockets for smoking materials as he went on.

"We took the easy way out. We solved that problem by keeping Snookums isolated. He has never met any animal except adult human beings. It would take an awful lot of explaining to make him understand the difference between, say, a chimpanzee and a man. Why should a hairy pelt and a relatively low intelligence make a chimp non-human? After all, some men are pretty hairy, and some are moronic.

"Present company excepted."

More laughter. Mike's opinion of Fitzhugh was beginning to go up. The man knew when to break pedantry with humor.

"Finally," Fitzhugh said, when the laughter had subsided, "we must ask what is meant by 'protecting his own existence.' Frankly, we've been driven frantic by that one. The little humanoid, caterpillar-track mechanism that we all tend to think of as Snookums isn't really Snookums, any more than a human being is a hand or an eye. Snookums wouldn't actually be threatening his own existence unless his brain—now in the hold of the *William Branchell*—is destroyed."

As Dr. Fitzhugh continued, Mike the Angel listened with about half an ear. His attention—and the attention of every man in the place—had been distracted by the entrance of Leda Crannon. She stepped in through a side door, walked over to Dr. Fitzhugh, and whispered something in his ear. He nodded, and she left again.

Fitzhugh, when he resumed his speech, was rather more hurried in his delivery.

"The whole thing can be summed up rather quickly.

"Point One: Snookums' brain contains the information that eight years of hard work have laboriously put into it. That information is more valuable than the whole cost of the *William Branchell*; it's worth billions. So the robot can't be disassembled, or the information would be lost.

"Point Two: Snookums' mind is a strictly logical one, but it is operating in a more than logical universe.

Consequently, it is unstable.

"Point Three: Snookums was built to conduct his own experiments. To forbid him to do that would be similar to beating a child for acting like a child; it would do serious harm to the mind. In Snookums' case, the randomity of the brain would exceed optimum, and the robot would become insane.

"Point Four: Emotion is not logical. Snookums can't handle it, except in a very limited way."

Fitzhugh had been making his points by tapping them off on his fingers with the stem of his unlighted pipe. Now he shoved the pipe back in his pocket and clasped his hands behind his back.

"It all adds up to this: Snookums *must* be allowed the freedom of the ship. At the same time, every one of us must be careful not to . . . to push the wrong buttons, as it were.

"So here are a few *don'ts*. Don't get angry with Snookums. That would be as silly as getting sore at a phonograph because it was playing music you didn't happen to like.

"Don't lie to Snookums. If your lies don't fit in with what he knows to be true—and they won't, believe me—he will reject the data. But it would confuse him, because he knows that humans don't lie.

"If Snookums asks you for data, qualify it—even if you know it to be true. Say: 'There may be an error in my knowledge of this data, but to the best of my knowledge . . .'

"Then go ahead and tell him.

"But if you absolutely don't know the answer, tell him so. Say: 'I don't have that data, Snookums.'

"Don't, unless you are . . .'"

He went on, but it was obvious that the officers and crew of the *William Branchell* weren't paying the attention they should. Every one of them was thinking dark gray thoughts. It was bad enough that they had to take out a ship like the *Brainchild*, untested and jerry-built as she was. Was it necessary to have an eight-hundred-pound, moron-genius child-machine running loose, too?

Evidently, it was.

"To wind it up," Fitzhugh said, "I imagine you are wondering why it's necessary to take Snookums off Earth. I can only tell you this: Snookums knows too much about nuclear energy."

Mike the Angel smiled grimly to himself. Ensign Vaneski had been right; Snookums was dangerous—not only to individuals, but to the whole planet.

Snookums, too, was a juvenile delinquent.

10

The *Branchild* lifted from Antarctica at exactly 2100 hours, Greenwich time. For three days the officers and men of the ship had worked as though they were the robots instead of their passenger—or cargo, depending on your point of view.

Supplies were loaded, and the great engine-generators checked and rechecked. The ship was ready to go less than two hours before take-off time.

The last passenger aboard was Snookums, although, in a more proper sense, he had always been aboard. The little robot rolled up to the elevator on his treads and was lifted into the body of the ship. Miss Crannon was waiting for him at the air lock, and Mike the Angel was standing by. Not that he had any particular interest in watching Snookums come aboard, but he did have a definite interest in Leda Crannon.

"Hello, honey," said Miss Crannon as Snookums rolled into the air lock. "Ready for your ride?"

"Yes, Leda," said Snookums in his contralto voice. He rolled up to her and took her hand. "Where is my room?"

"Come along; I'll show you in a minute. Do you remember Commander Gabriel?"

Snookums swiveled his head and regarded Mike.

"Oh yes. He tried to help me."

"Did you need help?" Mike growled in spite of himself.

"Yes. For my experiment. And you offered help. That was very nice. Leda says it is nice to help people."

Mike the Angel carefully refrained from asking Snookums if he thought he was people. For all Mike knew, he did.

Mike followed Snookums and Leda Crannon down the companionway.

"What did you do today, honey?" asked Leda.

"Mostly I answered questions for Dr. Fitzhugh," said Snookums. "He asked me thirty-eight questions. He said I was a great help. I'm nice, too."

"Sure you are, darling," said Miss Crannon.

"Ye gods," muttered Mike the Angel.

"What's the trouble, Commander?" the girl asked, widening her blue eyes.

"Nothing," said Mike the Angel, looking at her innocently with eyes that were equally blue. "Not a single solitary thing. Snookums is a sweet little tyke, isn't he?"

Leda Crannon gave him a glorious smile. "I think so. And a lot of fun, too."

Very seriously, Mike patted Snookums on his shiny steel skull. "How old are you, little boy?"

Leda Crannon's eyes narrowed, but Mike pretended not to notice while Snookums said: "Eight years, two months, one day, seven hours, thirty-three minutes and—ten seconds. But I am not a little boy. I am a robot."

Mike suppressed an impulse to ask him if he had informed Leda Crannon of that fact. Mike had been watching the girl for the past three days (at least, when he'd had the time to watch) and he'd been bothered by the girl's maternal attitude toward Snookums. She seemed to have wrapped herself up entirely in the little robot. Of course, that might simply be her method of avoiding Mike the Angel, but Mike didn't quite believe that.

"Come along to your room, dear," said Leda. Then she looked again at Mike. "If you'll wait just a moment, Commander," she said rather stiffly, "I'd like to talk to you."

Mike the Angel touched his forehead in a gentlemanly salute. "Later, perhaps, Miss Crannon. Right now, I have to go to the Power Section to prepare for take-off. We're really going to have fun lifting this brute against a full Earth gee without rockets."

"Later, then," she said evenly, and hurried off down the corridor with Snookums.

Mike headed the other way with a sigh of relief. As of right then, he didn't feel like being given an ear-reaming lecture by a beautiful redhead. He beetled it toward the Power Section.

Chief Powerman's Mate Multhaus was probably the only man in the crew who came close to being as big as Mike the Angel. Multhaus was two inches shorter than Mike's six-seven, but he weighed in at two-ninety. As a powerman, he was tops, and he gave the impression that, as far as power was concerned, he could have supplied the ship himself by turning the crank on a hand generator.

But neither Mike nor Multhaus approached the size of the Supply Officer, Lieutenant Keku. Keku was an absolute giant. Six-eight, three hundred fifty pounds, and very little of it fat.

When Mike the Angel opened the door of the Power Section's instrument room, he came upon a strange sight. Lieutenant Keku and Chief Multhaus were seated across a table from each other, each with his right elbow on the table, their right hands clasped. The muscles in both massive arms stood out beneath the scarlet tunics. Neither man was moving.

"Games, children?" asked Mike gently.

Whap! The chief's arm slammed to the table with a bang that sounded as if the table had shattered. Multhaus had allowed Mike's entrance to distract him, while Lieutenant Keku had held out just an instant longer.

Both men leaped to their feet, Multhaus valiantly trying not to nurse his bruised hand.

"Sorry, sir," said Multhaus. "We were just—"

"Ne' mind. I saw. Who usually wins?" Mike asked.

Lieutenant Keku grinned. "Usually he does, Commander. All this beef doesn't help much against a guy who really has pull. And Chief Multhaus has it."

Mike looked into the big man's brown eyes. "Try doing push-ups. With all your weight, it'd really put brawn into you. Sit down and light up. We've got time before take-off. That is, we do if Multhaus has everything ready for the check-off."

"I'm ready any time you are, sir," Multhaus said, easing himself into a chair.

"We'll have a cigarette and then run 'em through."

Keku settled his bulk into a chair and fired up a cigarette. Mike sat on the edge of the table.

"Philip Keku," Mike said musingly. "Just out of curiosity, what kind of a name is Keku?"

"Damfino," said the lieutenant. "Sounds Oriental, doesn't it?"

Mike looked the man over carefully, but rapidly. "But you're not Oriental—or at least, not much. You look Polynesian to me."

"Hit it right on the head, Commander. Hawaiian. My real name's Kekuanaoa, but nobody could pronounce it, so I shortened it to Keku when I came in the Service."

Mike gave a short laugh. "That accounts for your size. Kekuanaoa. A branch of the old Hawaiian royal family, as I recall."

"That's right." The big Hawaiian grinned. "I've got a kid sister that weighs as much as you. And my granddad kicked off at ninety-four weighing a comfortable four-ten."

"What'd he die of, sir?" Multhaus asked curiously.

"Concussion and multiple fractures. He slammed a Ford-Studebaker into a palm tree at ninety miles an hour. Crazy old ox; he was bigger than the dam' automobile."

The laughter of three big men filled the instrument room.

After a few more minutes of bull throwing, Keku ground out his cigarette and stood up. "I'd better get to my post; Black Bart will be calling down any minute."

At that instant the PA system came alive.

"Now hear this! Now hear this! Take-off in fifteen minutes! Take-off in fifteen minutes!"

Keku grinned, saluted Mike the Angel, and walked out the door.

Multhaus gazed after him, looking at the closed door. "A blinking prophet, Commander," he said. "A blinking prophet."

The take-off of the *Brainchild* was not so easy as it might have appeared to anyone who watched it from the outside. As far as the exterior observers were concerned, it seemed to lift into the air with a loud, thrumming noise, like a huge elevator rising in an invisible shaft.

It had been built in a deep pit in the polar ice, built around the huge cryotronic stack that was Snookums' brain. As it rose, electric motors slid back the roof that covered the pit, and the howling Antarctic winds roared around it.

Unperturbed, it went on rising.

Inside, Mike the Angel and Chief Multhaus watched worriedly as the meters wiggled their needles dangerously close to the overload mark. The thrumming of the ship as it fought its way up against the pull of Earth's gravity and through the Earth's magnetic field, using the fabric of space itself as the fulcrum against which it applied its power, was like the vibration of a note struck somewhere near the bottom of a piano keyboard, or the rumble of a contra bassoon.

As the intensity of the gravitational field decreased, the velocity of the ship increased—not linearly, but logarithmically. She shrieked through the upper atmosphere, quivering like a live thing, and emerged at last into relatively empty space. When she reached a velocity of a little over thirty miles per second—relative to the sun, and perpendicular to the solar ecliptic—Mike the Angel ordered her engines cut back to the lowest power possible which would still retain the one-gee interior gravity of the ship and keep the anti-acceleration fields intact.

11

"What I want to know," said Lieutenant Keku, "is, what kind of ship is this?"

Mike the Angel chuckled, and Lieutenant Mellon, the Medical Officer, grinned rather shyly. But young Ensign Vaneski looked puzzled.

"What do you mean, sir?" he asked the huge Hawaiian.

They were sitting over coffee in the officers' wardroom. Captain Quill, First Officer Jeffers, and Lieutenant Commander von Liegnitz were on the bridge, and Dr. Fitzhugh and Leda Crannon were down below, giving Snookums lessons.

Mike looked at Lieutenant Keku, waiting for him to answer Vaneski's question.

"What do I mean? Just what I said, Mister Vaneski. I want to know what kind of ship this is. It is obviously not a warship, so we can forget that classification. It is not an expeditionary ship; we're not outfitted for exploratory work. Is it a passenger vessel, then? No, because Dr. Fitzhugh and Miss Crannon are listed as 'civilian technical advisers' and are therefore legally part of the crew. I'm wondering if it might be a cargo vessel, though."

"Sure it is," said Ensign Vaneski. "The brain in Cargo Hold One is cargo, isn't it?"

"I'm not certain," Keku said thoughtfully, looking up at the overhead, as if the answer might be etched there in the metal. "Since it is built in as an intrinsic part of the ship, I don't know if it can be counted as cargo or not." He brought his gaze down to focus on Mike. "What do you think, Commander?"

Before Mike the Angel could answer, Ensign Vaneski broke in with: "But the brain is going to be removed when we get to our destination, isn't it? That makes this a cargo ship!" There was a note of triumph in his voice.

Lieutenant Keku's gaze didn't waver from Mike's face, nor did he say a word. For a boot ensign to interrupt like that was an impoliteness that Keku chose to ignore. He was waiting for Mike's answer as though Vaneski had said nothing.

But Mike the Angel decided he might as well play along with Keku's gag and still answer Vaneski. As a full commander, he could overlook Vaneski's impoliteness to his superiors without ignoring it as Keku was doing.

"Ah, but the brain *won't* be unloaded, Mister Vaneski," he said mildly. "The ship will be *dismantled*—which is an entirely different thing. I'm afraid you can't call it a cargo ship on those grounds."

Vaneski didn't say anything. His face had gone red and then white, as though he'd suddenly realized he'd committed a *faux pas*. He nodded his head a little, to show he understood, but he couldn't seem to find his voice.

To cover up Vaneski's emotional dilemma, Mike addressed the Medical Officer. "What do you think, Mister Mellon?"

Mellon cleared his throat. "Well—it seems to me," he said in a dry, serious tone, "that this is really a medical ship."

Mike blinked. Keku raised his eyebrows. Vaneski swallowed and jerked his eyes away from Mike's face to look at Mellon—but still he didn't say anything.

"Elucidate, my dear Doctor," said Mike with interest.

"I diagnose it as a physician," Mellon said in the same dry, earnest tone. "Snookums, we have been told, is too dangerous to be permitted to remain on Earth. I take this to mean that he is potentially capable of doing something that would either harm the planet itself or a majority—if not all—of the people on it." He picked up his cup of coffee and took a sip. Nobody interrupted him.

"Snookums has, therefore," he continued, "been removed from Earth in order to protect the health of that planet, just as one would remove a potentially malignant tumor from a human body.

"This is a medical ship. Q.E.D." And only then did he smile.

"Aw, now . . ." Vaneski began. Then he shut his mouth again.

With an inward smile, Mike realized that Ensign Vaneski had been taking seriously an argument that was strictly a joke.

"Mister Mellon," Mike said, "you win." He hadn't realized that Mellon's mind could work on that level.

"Hold," said Lieutenant Keku, raising a hand. "I yield to no one in my admiration for the analysis given by our good doctor; indeed, my admiration knows no bounds. But I insist we hear from Commander Gabriel before we adjourn."

"Not me," Mike said, shaking his head. "I know when I'm beaten." He'd been going to suggest that the *Brainchild* was a training ship, from Snookums' "learning" periods, but that seemed rather obvious and puerile now.

He glanced at his watch, saw the time, and stood up. "Excuse me, gentlemen; I have things to do." He had an appointment to talk to Leda Crannon, but he had no intention of broadcasting it.

As he closed the wardroom door, he heard Ensign Vaneski's voice saying: "I *still* say this should be classified as a cargo ship."

Mike sighed as he strode on down the companionway. The ensign was, of course, absolutely correct—which was the sad part about it, really. Oh well, what the hell.

Leda Crannon had agreed to have coffee with Mike in the office suite she shared with Dr. Fitzhugh. Mike had had one cup in the officers' wardroom, but even if he'd had a dozen he'd have been willing to slosh down a dozen more to talk to Leda Crannon. It was not, he insisted to himself, that he was in love with the girl, but she had intelligence and personality in addition to her striking beauty.

Furthermore, she had given Mike the Angel a dressing-down that had been quite impressive. She had not at all cared for the remarks he had made when Snookums was being loaded aboard—patting him on the head and asking him his age, for instance—and had told him so in no uncertain terms. Mike, feeling sheepish and knowing he was guilty, had accepted the tongue-lashing and tendered an apology.

And she had smiled and said: "All right. Forget it. I'm sorry I got mad."

He knew he wasn't the only man aboard who was interested in Leda. Jakob von Liegnitz, all Teutonic masterfulness and Old World suavity, had obviously made a favorable impression on her. Lew Mellon was often seen in deep philosophical discussions with her, his eyes never leaving her face and his earnest voice low and confidential. Both of them had known her longer than he had, since they'd both been stationed at Chilblains Base.

Mike the Angel didn't let either of them worry him. He had enough confidence in his own personality and abilities to be able to take his own tack no matter which way the wind blew.

Blithely opening the door of the office, Mike the Angel stepped inside with a smile on his lips.

"Ah, good afternoon, Commander Gabriel," said Dr. Morris Fitzhugh.

Mike kept the smile on his face. "Leda here?"

Fitzhugh chuckled. "No. Some problems came up with Snookums. She'll be in session for an hour yet. She asked me to convey her apologies." He gestured toward the coffee urn. "But the coffee's all made, so you may as well have a cup."

Mike was thankful he had not had a dozen cups in the wardroom. "I don't mind if I do, Doctor." He sat down while Fitzhugh poured a cup.

"Cream? Sugar?"

"Black, thanks," Mike said.

There was an awkward silence for a few seconds while Mike sipped at the hot, black liquid. Then Mike said, "Dr. Fitzhugh, you said, at the briefing back on Earth, that Snookums knows too much about nuclear energy.

Can you be more specific than that, or is it too hush-hush?"

Fitzhugh took out his briar and began filling it as he spoke. "We don't want this to get out to the general public, of course," he said thoughtfully, "but, as a ship's officer, you can be told. I believe some of your fellow officers know already, although we'd rather it wasn't discussed in general conversation, even among the officers."

Mike nodded wordlessly.

"Very well, then." Fitzhugh gave the tobacco a final shove with his thumb. "As a power engineer, you should be acquainted with the 'pinch effect,' eh?"

It was a rhetorical question. The "pinch effect" had been known for over a century. A jet of highly ionized gas, moving through a magnetic field of the proper structure, will tend to pinch down, to become narrower, rather than to spread apart, as a jet of ordinary gas does. As the science of magnetohydrodynamics had progressed, the effect had become more and more controllable, enabling scientists to force the nuclei of hydrogen, for instance, closer and closer together. At the end of the last century, the Bending Converter had almost wrecked the economy of the entire world, since it gave to the world a source of free energy. Sam Bending's "little black box" converted ordinary water into helium and oxygen and energy—plenty of energy. A Bending Converter could be built relatively cheaply and for small-power uses—such as powering a ship or automobile or manufacturing plant—could literally run on air, since the moisture content of ordinary air was enough to power the converter itself with plenty of power left over.

Overnight, all previous forms of power generation had become obsolete. Who would buy electric power when he could generate his own for next to nothing? Billions upon billions of dollars worth of generating equipment were rendered valueless. The great hydro-electric dams, the hundreds of steam turbines, the heavy-metal atomic reactors—all useless for power purposes. The value of the stock in those companies dropped to zero and stayed there. The value of copper metal fell like a bomb, with almost equally devastating results—for there was no longer any need for the millions of miles of copper cable that linked the power plants with the consumer.

The Depression of 1929-42 couldn't even begin to compare with The Great Depression of 1986-2000. Every civilized nation on Earth had been hit and hit hard. The resulting governmental collapses would have made the disaster even more complete had not the then Secretary General of the UN, Perrot of Monaco, grabbed the reins of government. Like the Americans Franklin Roosevelt and Abraham Lincoln, he had forced through unconstitutional bills and taken extra-constitutional powers. And, like those Americans, he had not done it for personal gain, but to preserve the society. He had not succeeded in preserving the old society, of course, but he had built, almost single-handedly, a world government—a new society on the foundations of the old.

All these thoughts ran through Mike the Angel's mind. He wondered if Snookums had discovered something that would be as much a disaster to the world economy as the Bending Converter had been.

Fitzhugh got out his miniature flame thrower and

puffed his pipe alight. "Snookums," he said, "has discovered a method of applying the pinch effect to lithium hydride. It's a batch reaction rather than a flow reaction such as the Bending Converter uses. But it's as simple to build as a Bending Converter."

"Jesus," said Mike the Angel softly.

Lithium hydride. LiH. An atom of hydrogen to every atom of lithium. If a hydrogen nucleus is driven into the lithium nucleus with sufficient force, the results are simple:

$$Li^7 + H^1 \blacktriangleright {}_2He^4 + energy$$

An atom of lithium-7 plus an atom of hydrogen-1 yields two atoms of helium-4 and plenty of energy. One gram of lithium hydride would give nearly fifty-eight kilowatt-hours of energy in one blast. A pound of the stuff would be the equivalent of nearly seven *tons* of TNT.

In addition, it was a nice, clean bomb. Nothing but helium, radiation, and heat. In the early nineteen fifties, such a bomb had been constructed by surrounding the LiH with a fission bomb—the so-called "implosion" technique. But all that heavy metal around the central reaction created all kinds of radioactive residues which had a tendency to scatter death for hundreds of miles around.

Now, suppose a man had a pair of tweezers small enough to pick up a single molecule of lithium hydride and pinch the two nuclei together. Of course, the idea is ridiculous—that is, the tweezer part is. But if the pinch could be done in some other way . . .

Snookums had done it.

"Homemade atomic bombs in your back yard or basement lab," said Mike the Angel.

Fitzhugh nodded emphatically. "Exactly. We can't let that technique out until we've found a way to keep people from doing just that. The UN Government has inspection techniques that prevent anyone from building the conventional types of thermonuclear bombs, but not the pinch bomb."

Mike the Angel thought over what Dr. Fitzhugh had said. Then he said: "That's not all of it. Antarctica is isolated enough to keep that knowledge secret for a long time—at least until safeguards could be set up. Why take Snookums off Earth?"

"Snookums himself is dangerous," Fitzhugh said. "He has a built-in 'urge' to experiment—to get data. We can keep him from making experiments that we know will be dangerous by giving him the data, so that the urge doesn't operate. But if he's on the track of something totally new . . .

"Well, you can see what we're up against." He thoughtfully blew a cloud of smoke. "We think he may be on the track of the total annihilation of matter."

A dead silence hung in the air. The ultimate, the superatomic bomb. Theoretically, the idea had been approached only in the assumption of contact between ordinary matter and anti-matter, with the two canceling each other completely to give nothing but energy. Such a bomb would be nearly fifty thousand times as powerful as the lithium-hydride pinch bomb. That much energy, released in a few millimicroseconds, would make the standard H-bomb look like a candle flame on a foggy night.

The LiH pinch bomb could be controlled. By using

just a little of the stuff, it would be possible to limit the destruction to a neighborhood, or even a single block. A total-annihilation bomb would be much harder to control. The total annihilation of a single atom of hydrogen would yield over a thousandth of an erg, and matter just doesn't come in much smaller packages than that.

"You see," said Fitzhugh, "we *had* to get him off Earth."

"Either that or stop him from experimenting," Mike said. "And I assume that wouldn't be good for Snookums."

"To frustrate Snookums would be to destroy all the work we have put into him. His circuits would tend to exceed optimum randomness, and that would mean, in human terms, that he would be insane—and therefore worthless. As a machine, Snookums is worth eighteen billion dollars. The information we have given him, plus the deductions and computations he has made from that information, is worth . . ." He shrugged his shoulders. "Who knows? How can a price be put on knowledge?"

12

The *William Branchell*—dubbed *Brainchild*—fled Earth at ultralight velocity, while officers, crew, and technical advisers settled down to routine. The only thing that disturbed that routine was one particularly restless part of the ship's cargo.

Snookums was a snoop.

Cut off from the laboratories which had been provided for his special work at Chilblains, he proceeded to interest himself in the affairs of the human beings which surrounded him. Until his seventh year, he had been confined to the company of only a small handful of human beings. Even while the *William Branchell* was being built, he hadn't been allowed any more freedom than was absolutely necessary to keep him from being frustrated.

Even so, he had developed an interest in humans. Now he was being allowed full rein in his data-seeking circuits, and he chose to investigate, not the physical sciences, but the study of Mankind. Since the proper study of Mankind is Man, Snookums proceeded to study the people on the ship.

Within three days the officers had evolved a method of Snookums-evasion.

Lieutenant Commander Jakob von Liegnitz sat in the officers' wardroom of the *Brainchild* and shuffled a deck of cards with expert fingers.

He was a medium-sized man, five-eleven or so, with a barrel chest, broad shoulders, a narrow waist, and lean hips. His light brown hair was worn rather long, and its straight strands seemed to cling tightly to his skull. His gray eyes had a perpetual half-squint that made him look either sleepy or angry, depending on what the rest of his broad face was doing.

He dealt himself out a board of Four Cards Up and had gone through about half a pack when Mike the Angel came in with Lieutenant Keku.

"Hello, Jake," said Keku. "What's to do?"

"Get out two more decks," said Mike the Angel, "and we can all play solitaire."

Von Liegnitz looked up sleepily. "I could probably think of duller things, Mike, but not just immediately. How about bridge?"

"We'll need a fourth," said Keku. "How about Pete?"

Mike the Angel shook his head. "Black Bart is sleeping—taking his beauty nap. So Pete has the duty. How about young Vaneski? He's not a bad partner."

"He is out, too," said von Liegnitz. "He also is on duty."

Mike the Angel lifted an inquisitive eyebrow. "Something busted? Why should the Maintenance Officer be on duty right now?"

"He is maintaining," said von Liegnitz with deliberate dignity, "peace and order around here. He is now performing the duty of Answerman-in-Chief. He's very good at it."

Mike grinned. "Snookums?"

Von Liegnitz scooped the cards off the table and began shuffling them. "Exactly. As long as Snookums gets his questions answered, he keeps himself busy. Our young boot ensign has been assigned to the duty of keeping that mechanical Peeping Tom out of our hair for an hour. By then, it will be lunch time." He cleared his throat. "We still need a fourth."

"If you ask me," said Lieutenant Keku, "we need a fifth. Let's play poker instead."

Jakob von Liegnitz nodded and offered the cards for a cut.

"Deal 'em," said Mike the Angel.

A few minutes less than an hour later, Ensign Vaneski slid open the door to the wardroom and was greeted by a triune chorus of hellos.

"Sirs," said Vaneski with pseudo formality, "I have done my duty, exhausting as it was. I demand satisfaction."

Lieutenant Keku, upon seeing Mike the Angel dealt a second eight, flipped over his up cards and folded.

"Satisfaction?" he asked the ensign.

Vaneski nodded. "One hand of showdown for five clams. I have been playing encyclopedia for that hunk of animated machinery for an hour. That's above and beyond the call of duty."

"Raise a half," said Mike the Angel.

"Call," said von Liegnitz.

"Three eights," said Mike, flipping his hole card.

Von Liegnitz shrugged, folded his cards, and watched solemnly while Mike pulled in the pot.

"Vaneski wants to play showdown for a fiver," said Keku.

Mike the Angel frowned at the ensign for a moment, then relaxed and nodded. "Not my game," he said, "but if the Answerman wants a chance to catch up, it's okay with me."

The four men each tossed a five spot into the center of the table and then cut for deal. Mike got it and started dealing—five cards, face up, for the pot.

When three cards apiece had been dealt, young Vaneski was ahead with a king high. On the fourth round he grinned when he got a second king and Mike dealt himself an ace.

On the fifth round Vaneski got a three, and his face froze as Mike dealt himself a second ace.

Mike reached for the twenty.

"You deal yourself a mean hand, Commander," said Vaneski evenly.

Mike glanced at him sharply, but there was only a wry grin on the young ensign's face.

"Luck of the idiot," said Mike as he pocketed the twenty. "It's time for lunch."

"Next time," said Keku firmly, "I'll take the Answerman watch, Mike. You and this kraut are too lucky for me."

"If I lose any more to the Angel," von Liegnitz said calmly, "I will be a very sour kraut. But right now, I'm quite hungry."

Mike prowled around the Power Section that afternoon with a worry nagging at the back of his mind. He couldn't exactly put his finger on what was bothering him, and he finally put it down to just plain nerves.

And then he began to feel something—physically.

Within thirty seconds after it began, long before most of the others had noticed it, Mike the Angel recognized it for what it was. Half a minute after that, everyone aboard could feel it.

A two-cycle-per-second beat note is inaudible to the human ear. If the human tympanum can't wiggle any faster than that, the auditory nerves refuse to transmit the message. The wiggle has to be three or four octaves above that before the nerves will have anything to do with it. But if the beat note has enough energy in it, a man doesn't have to hear it—he can *feel* it.

The bugs weren't all out of the *Brainchild*, by any means, and the men knew it. She had taken a devil of a strain on the take-off, and something was about due to weaken.

It was the external field around the hull that had decided to goof off this time. It developed a nice, unpleasant two-cycle throb that threatened to shake the ship apart. It built up rapidly and then leveled off, giving everyone aboard the feeling that his lunch and his stomach would soon part company.

The crew was used to it. They'd been on shakedown cruises before, and they knew that on an interstellar vessel the word "shakedown" can have a very literal meaning. The beat note wasn't dangerous, but it wasn't pleasant, either.

Within five minutes everybody aboard had the galloping collywobbles and the twittering jitters.

Mike and his power crew all knew what to do. They took their stations and started to work. They had barely started when Captain Quill's voice came over the intercom.

"Power Section, this is the bridge. How long before

we stop this beat note?''

"No way of telling, sir," said Mike, without taking his eyes off the meter bank. "Check A-77," he muttered in an aside to Multhaus.

"Can you give me a prognosis?" persisted Quill.

Mike frowned. This wasn't like Black Bart. He knew what the prognosis was as well as Mike did. "Actually, sir, there's no way of knowing. The old *Gainsway* shook like this for eight days before they spotted the tubes that were causing a four-cycle beat."

"Why can't we spot it right off?" Quill asked.

Mike got it then. Fitzhugh was listening in. Quill wanted Mike the Angel to substantiate his own statements to the roboticist.

"There are sixteen generator tubes in the hull—two at each end of the four diagonals of an imaginary cube surrounding the ship. At least two of them are out of phase; that means that every one of them may have to be balanced against every other one, and that would make a hundred and twenty checks. It will take ten minutes if we hit it lucky and find the bad tubes in the first two tries, and about twenty hours if we hit on the last try.

"That, of course, is presuming that there are only two out. If there are three . . ." He let it hang.

Mike grinned as Dr. Morris Fitzhugh's voice came over the intercom, confirming his diagnosis of the situation.

"Isn't there any other way?" asked Fitzhugh worriedly. "Can't we stop the ship and check them, so that we won't be subjected to this?"

" 'Fraid not," answered Mike. "In the first place, cutting the external field would be dangerous, if not deadly. The abrupt deceleration wouldn't be good for us, even with the internal field operating. In the second place, we couldn't check the field tubes if they weren't operating. You can't tell a bad tube just by looking at it. They'd still have to be balanced against each other, and that would take the same amount of time as it is going to take anyway, and with the same effects on the ship. I'm sorry, but we'll just have to put up with it."

"Well, for Heaven's sake do the best you can," Fitzhugh said in a worried voice. "This beat is shaking Snookums' brain. God knows what damage it may do unless it's stopped within a very few minutes!"

"I'll do the best I can," said Mike the Angel carefully. "So will every man in my crew. But about all anyone can do is wish us luck and let us work."

"Yes," said Dr. Fitzhugh slowly. "Yes, I understand. Thank you, Commander."

Mike the Angel nodded curtly and went back to work.

Things weren't bad enough as they were. They had to get worse. The *Brainchild* had been built too fast, and in too unorthodox a manner. The steady two-cycle throb did more damage than it would normally have done aboard a non-experimental ship.

Twelve minutes after the throb started, a feeder valve in the pre-induction energy chamber developed a positive-feedback oscillation that threatened to blow out the whole preinduction stage unless it was damped. The search for the out-of-phase external field tubes had to be dropped while the more dangerous flaw was tackled.

Multhaus plugged in an emergency board and began to compensate by hand while the others searched frantically for the trouble.

Hand compensation of feeder-valve oscillation is pure intuition; if you wait until the meters show that damping is necessary, it may be too late—you have to second-guess the machine and figure out what's coming *before* it happens and compensate then. You not only have to judge time, but magnitude; overcompensation is ruinous, too.

Multhaus, the Chief Powerman's Mate, sat behind the emergency board, a vernier dial in each hand and both eyes on an oscilloscope screen. His red, beefy face was corded and knotted with tension, and his skin glistened with oily perspiration. He didn't say a word, and his fingers barely moved as he held a green line reasonably steady on that screen.

Mike the Angel, using unangelic language in a steady, muttering stream, worked to find the circuit that held the secret of the ruinous feedback tendency, while other powermen plugged and unplugged meter jacks, flipped switches, and juggled tools.

In the midst of all this, in rolled Snookums.

Whether Snookums knew that his own existence was in danger is problematical. Like the human brain, his own had no pain or sensory circuits within it; in addition, his knowledge of robotics was small—he didn't even know that his brain was in Cargo Hold One. He thought it was in his head, if he thought about it at all.

Nonetheless, he knew *something* was wrong, and as soon as his "curiosity" circuits were activated, he set out in search of the trouble, his little treads rolling at high speed.

Leda Crannon saw him heading down a companionway and called after him. "Where are you going, Snookums?"

"Looking for data," answered Snookums, slowing a little.

"Wait! I'll come with you!"

Leda Crannon knew perfectly well what effect the throb might have on Snookums' brain, and when something cracked, she wanted to see what effect it might have on the behavior of the little robot. Like a hound after a fox, she followed him through the corridors of the ship.

Up companionways and down, in and out of storerooms, staterooms, control rooms, and washrooms Snookums scurried, oblivious to the consternation that sometimes erupted at his sudden appearance. At certain selected spots, Snookums would stop, put his metal arms on floors and walls, pause, and then go zooming off in another direction with Leda Crannon only paces behind him, trying to explain to crewmen as best she could.

If Snookums had been capable of emotion—and Leda Crannon was not as sure as the roboticists that he wasn't—she would have sworn that he was having the time of his life.

Seventeen minutes after the throb had begun, Snookums rolled into Power Section and came to a halt. Something else was wrong.

At first he just stopped by the door and soaked in data. Mike's muttering; the clipped, staccato conversation of the power crew; the noises of the tools; the deep throb of the ship itself; the underlying oddness of the engine vibrations—all these were fed into his microphonic ears. The scene itself was transmitted to his brain and recorded. The cryotronic maze in the depths of the ship chewed the whole thing over. Snookums acted.

Leda Crannon, who had lost ground in trying to keep

up with Snookums' whirling treads, came to the door of Power Section too late to stop the robot's entrance. She didn't dare call out, because she knew that to do so would interrupt the men's vital work. All she could do was lean against the doorjamb and try to catch her breath.

Snookums rolled over to the board where Multhaus was sitting and watched over his shoulder for perhaps thirty seconds. The crewmen eyed him, but they were much too busy to do anything. Besides, they were used to his presence by this time.

Then, in one quick tour of the room, Snookums glanced at every meter in the place. Not just at the regular operating meters, but also at the meters in the testing equipment that the power crew had jack-plugged in.

Mike the Angel looked around as he heard the soft purring of the caterpillar treads. His glance took in both Snookums and Leda Crannon, who was still gasping at the door. He watched Leda for the space of three deep breaths, tore his eyes away, looked at what Snookums was doing, then said: "Get him out of here!" in a stage whisper to Leda.

Snookums was looking over the notations on the meter readings for the previous few minutes. He had simply picked them up from the desk where one of the computermen was working and scanned them rapidly before handing them back.

Before Leda could say anything, Snookums rolled over to Mike the Angel and said: "Check the lead between the 391-JF and the big DK-37. I think you'll find that the piping is in phase with the two-cycle note, and it's become warped and stretched. It's about half a millimeter off—plus or minus a tenth. The pulse is reaching the DK-37 about four degrees off, and the gate is closing before it all gets through. That's forcing the regulator circuit to overcompensate, and . . ."

Mike didn't listen to any more. He didn't know whether Snookums knew what he was talking about or not, but he did know that the thing the robot had mentioned would have had just such an effect.

Mike strode rapidly across the room and flipped up the shield housing the assembly Snookums had mentioned. The lead was definitely askew.

Mike the Angel snapped orders, and the power crewmen descended on the scene of the trouble.

Snookums went right on delivering his interpretation of the data, but everyone ignored him while they worked. Being ignored didn't bother Snookums in the least.

". . . and that, in turn, is making the feeder valve field oscillate," he finished up, nearly five minutes later.

Mike was glad that Snookums had pinpointed the trouble first and then had gone on to show why the defect was causing the observed result. He could just as easily have started with the offending oscillation and reached the bit about the faulty lead at the end of his speech, except that he had been built to do it the other way around. Snookums made the deduction in his superfast mind and then reeled it off backward, as it were, going from conclusion to premises.

Otherwise, he might have been too late.

The repair didn't take long, once Snookums had found just what needed repairing. When the job was over, Mike the Angel wiped his hands on a rag and stood up.

"Thanks, Snookums," he said honestly. "You've been a great help."

Snookums said: "I am smiling. Because I am pleased."

There was no way for him to smile with a steel face, but Mike got the idea.

Mike turned to the Chief Powerman's Mate. "Okay, Multhaus, shut it off. She's steady now."

Multhaus just sat there, surrounded by a wall of concentration, his hands still on the verniers, his eyes still on the screen. He didn't move.

Mike flipped off the switch. "Come on, Multhaus, snap to. We've still got that beat note to worry about."

Multhaus blinked dizzily as the green line vanished from his sight. He jerked his hands off the verniers, and then smiled sheepishly. He had been sitting there waiting for that green line to move a full minute after the input signal had ceased.

"Happy hypnosis," said Mike. "Let's get back to finding out which of those tubes in the hull is giving the external field the willies."

Snookums, who had been listening carefully, rolled up and said, "Generator tubes three, four, and thirteen. Three is out of phase by—"

"You can tell us later, Snookums," Mike interrupted rapidly. "Right now, we'll get to work on those tubes. You were right once; I hope you're right again."

Again the power crew swung into action.

Within five minutes Mike and Multhaus were making the proper adjustments on the external field circuits to adjust for the wobbling of the output.

The throb wavered. It wobbled around, going up to

two-point-seven cycles and dropping back to one-point-four, then climbing again. All the time, it was dropping in magnitude, until finally it could no longer be felt. Finally, it dropped suddenly to a low of point-oh-five cycles, hovered there for a moment, then vanished altogether.

"By the beard of my sainted maiden aunt," said Chief Multhaus in awe. "A three-tube offbeat solved in less than half an hour! If that isn't a record, I'll dye my uniform black and join the Chaplains' Corps."

Leda Crannon, looking tired but somehow pleased, said softly: "May I come in?"

Mike the Angel grinned. "Sure. Maybe you can—"

The intercom clicked on. "Power Section, this is the bridge." It was Black Bart. "Are my senses playing me false, or have you stopped that beat note?"

"All secure, sir," said Mike the Angel. "The system is stable now."

"How many tubes were goofing?"

"Three of them."

"*Three*!" There was astonishment in the captain's voice. "How did you ever solve a three-tube beat in that short a time?"

Mike the Angel grinned up at the eye in the wall.

"Nothing to it, sir," he said. "A child could have done it."

13

Leda Crannon sat down on the edge of the bunk in Mike the Angel's stateroom, accepted the cigarette and light that Mike had proffered, and waited while Mike poured a couple of cups of coffee from the insul-jug on his desk.

"I wish I could offer you something stronger, but I'm not much of a drinker myself, so I don't usually take advantage of the officer's prerogative to smuggle liquor aboard," he said as he handed her the cup.

She smiled up at him. "That's all right; I rarely drink, and when I do, it's either wine or a *very* diluted highball. Right now, this coffee will do me more good."

Mike heard footsteps coming down the companionway. He glanced out through the door, which he had deliberately left open. Ensign Vaneski walked by, glanced in, grinned, and went on his way. The kid had good sense, Mike thought. He hoped any other passersby would stay out while he talked to Leda.

"Does a thing like that happen often?" the girl asked. "Not the fast solution; I mean the beat note."

"No," said Mike the Angel. "Once the system is stabilized, the tubes tend to keep each other in line. But because of that very tendency, an offbeat tube won't show itself for a while. The system tries to keep the bad ones in phase in spite of themselves. But eventually one of them sort of rebels, and that frees any of the others that are offbeat, so the bad ones all show at once and we can spot them. When we get all the bad ones adjusted, the system remains stable for the operating life of the system."

"And that's the purpose of a shakedown cruise?"

"One of the reasons," agreed Mike. "If the tubes are going to act up, they'll do it in the first five hundred operating hours—except in unusual cases. That's one of the things that bothered me about the way this crate was hashed together."

Her blue eyes widened. "I thought this was a well-built ship."

"Oh, it is, it is—all things considered. It isn't dangerous, if that's what you're worried about. But it sure as the devil is expensively wasteful."

She nodded and sipped at her coffee. "I know that. But I don't see any other way it could have been done."

"Neither do I, right off the bat," Mike admitted. He took a good swallow of the hot liquid in his cup and said: "I wanted to ask you two questions. First, what was it that Snookums was doing just before he came into the Power Section? Black Bart said he'd been galloping all over the ship, with you at his heels."

Her infectious smile came back. "He was playing seismograph. He was simply checking the intensity of the vibrations at different points in the ship. That gave him part of the data he needed to tell you which of the tubes were acting up."

126

"I'm beginning to think," said Mike, "that we'll have to start building a big brain aboard every ship—that is, if we can learn enough about such monsters from Snookums."

"What was the other question?" Leda asked.

"Oh . . . Well, I was wondering just why you are connected with this project. What does a psychologist have to do with robots? If you'll pardon my ignorance."

This time she laughed softly, and Mike thought dizzily of the gay chiming of silver bells. He clamped down firmly on the romantic wanderings of his mind as she started her explanation.

"I'm a specialist in child psychology, Mike. Actually, I was hired as an experiment—or, rather, as the result of a wild guess that happened to work. You see, the first two times Snookums' brain was activated, the circuits became disoriented."

"You mean," said Mike the Angel, "they went nuts."

She laughed again. "Don't let Fitz hear you say that. He'll tell you that 'the circuits exceeded their optimum randomity limit.' "

Mike grinned, remembering the time he had driven a robot brain daffy by bluffing it at poker. "How did that happen?"

"Well, we don't know all the details, but it seems to have something to do with the slow recovery rate that's necessary for learning. Do you know anything about Lagerglocke's Principle?"

"Fitzhugh mentioned something about it in the briefing we got before take-off. Something about a bit of learning being an inelastic rebound."

"That's it. You take a steel ball, for instance, and

drop it on a steel plate from a height of three or four feet. It bounces—almost perfect elasticity. The next time you drop it, it does the same thing. It hasn't learned anything.

"But if you drop a lead ball, it doesn't bounce as much, and it will flatten at the point of contact. *The next time it falls on that flat side, its behavior will be different*. It has learned something."

Mike rubbed the tip of an index finger over his chin. "These illustrations are analogues of the human mind?"

"That's right. Some people have minds like steel balls. They can learn, but you have to hit them pretty hard to make them do it. On the other hand, some people have minds like glass balls: They can't learn at all. If you hit them hard enough to make a real impression, they simply shatter."

"All right. Now what has this got to do with you and Snookums?"

"Patience, boy, patience," Leda said with a grin. "Actually, the lead-ball analogy is much too simple. An intelligent mind has to have time to partially recover, you see. Hit it with too many shocks, one right after another, and it either collapses or refuses to learn or both.

"The first two times the brain was activated, the roboticists just began feeding data into the thing as though it were an ordinary computing machine. They were forcing it to learn too fast; they weren't giving it time to recover from the shock of learning.

"Just as in the human being, there is a difference between a robot's brain and a robot's mind. The *brain* is a physical thing—a bunch of cryotrons in a helium bath.

But the *mind* is the sum total of all the data and reaction patterns and so forth that have been built into the brain or absorbed by it.

"The brain didn't have an opportunity to recover from the learning shocks when the data was fed in too fast, so the mind cracked. It couldn't take it. The robot went insane.

"Each time, the roboticists had to deactivate the brain, drain it of all data, and start over. After the second time, Dr. Fitzhugh decided they were going about it wrong, so they decided on a different tack."

"I see," said Mike the Angel. "It had to be taught slowly, like a child."

"Exactly," said Leda. "And who would know more about teaching a child than a child psychologist?" she added brightly.

Mike looked down at his coffee cup, watching the slight wavering of the surface as it broke up the reflected light from the glow panels. He had invited this girl down to his stateroom (he told himself) to get information about Snookums. But now he realized that information about the girl herself was far more important.

"How long have you been working with Snookums?" he asked, without looking up from his coffee.

"Over eight years," she said.

Then Mike looked up. "You know, you hardly look old enough. You don't look much older than twenty-five."

She smiled—a little shyly, Mike thought. "As Snookums says, 'You're nice.' I'm twenty-six."

"And you've been working with Snookums since you were eighteen?"

"Uh-huh." She looked, very suddenly, much

younger than even the twenty-five Mike had guessed at. She seemed to be more like a somewhat bashful teen-ager who had been educated in a convent. "I was what they call an 'exceptional child.' My mother died when I was seven, and Dad . . . well, he just didn't know what to do with a baby girl, I guess. He was a kind man, and I think he really loved me, but he just didn't know what to do with me. So when the tests showed that I was . . . brighter . . . than the average, he put me in a special school in Italy. Said he didn't want my mind cramped by being forced to conform to the mental norm. Maybe he even believed that himself.

"And, too, he didn't approve of public education. He had a lot of odd ideas.

"Anyway, I saw him during summer vacations and went to school the rest of the year. He took me all over the world when I was with him, and the instructors were pretty wonderful people; I'm not sorry that I was brought up that way. It was a little different from the education that most children have, but it gave me a chance to use my mind."

"I know the school," said Mike the Angel. "That's the one under the Cesare Alfieri Institute in Florence?"

"That's it; did you go there?" There was an odd, eager look in her eyes.

Mike shook his head. "Nope. But a friend of mine did. Ever know a guy named Paulvitch?"

She squealed with delight, as though she'd been playfully pinched. "Sir Gay? You mean Serge Paul-vitch, the Fiend of Florence?" She pronounced the name properly: "*Sair-gay,*" instead of "surge," as too many people were prone to do.

"Sounds like the same man," Mike admitted,

grinning. "As evil-looking as Satanas himself?"

"That's Sir Gay, all right. Half the girls were scared of him, and I think *all* the boys were. He's about three years older than I am, I guess."

"Why call him Sir Gay?" Mike asked. "Just because of his name?"

"Partly. And partly because he was always such a gentleman. A real *nice* guy, if you know what I mean. Do you know him well?"

"*Know* him? Hell, I couldn't run my business without him."

"Your business?" She blinked. "But he works for—" Then her eyes became very wide, her mouth opened, and she pointed an index finger at Mike. "Then you . . . you're Mike the Angel! M. R. Gabriel! Sure!" She started laughing. "I never connected it up! My golly, my golly! I thought you were just another Space Service commander! Mike the Angel! Well, I'll be damned!"

She caught her breath. "I'm sorry. I was just so surprised, that's all. Are you really *the* M. R. Gabriel, of M. R. Gabriel, Power Design?"

Mike was as close to being nonplused as he cared to be. "Sure," he said. "You mean you didn't know?"

She shook her head. "No. I thought Mike the Angel was about sixty years old, a crotchety old genius behind a desk, as eccentric as a comet's orbit, and wealthier than Croesus. You're just not what I pictured, that's all."

"Just wait a few more decades," Mike said, laughing. "I'll try to live up to my reputation."

"So you're Serge's boss. How is he? I haven't seen him since I was sixteen."

"He's grown a beard," said Mike.

"No!"

"Fact."

"My God, how horrible!" She put her hand over her eyes in mock horror.

"Let's talk about you," said Mike. "You're much prettier than Serge Paulvitch."

"Well, I should hope so! But really, there's nothing to tell. I went to school. B.S. at fourteen, M.S. at sixteen, Ph.D. at eighteen. Then I went to work for C.C. of E., and I've been there ever since. I've never been engaged, I've never been married, and I'm still a virgin. Anything else?"

"No runs, no hits, no errors," said Mike the Angel.

She grinned back impishly. "I haven't been up to bat yet, Commander Gabriel."

"Then I suggest you grab some sort of club to defend yourself, because I'm going to be in there pitching."

The smile on her face faded, to be replaced by a look that was neither awe nor surprise, but partook of both.

"You really mean that, don't you?" she asked him in a hushed voice.

"I do," said Mike the Angel.

Commander Peter Jeffers was in the Control Bridge when Mike the Angel stepped in through the door. Jeffers was standing with his back to the door, facing the bank of instruments that gave him a general picture of the condition of the whole ship.

Overhead, the great dome of the ship's nose allowed the gleaming points of light from the star field ahead to shine down on those beneath through the heavy, transparent shield of the cast transite and the invisible screen on the external field.

132

Mike walked over and tapped Pete Jeffers on the shoulder.

"Busy?"

Jeffers turned around slowly and grinned. "Hullo, old soul. Naw, I ain't busy. Nothin' outside but stars, and we don't figger on gettin' too close to 'em right off the bat. What's the beef?"

"I have," said Mike the Angel succinctly, "goofed."

Jeffers' keen eyes swept analytically over Mike the Angel's face. "You want a drink? I snuck a spot o' brandy aboard, and just by purity ole coincidence, there's a bottle right over there in the speaker housing." Without waiting for an answer, he turned away from Mike and walked toward the cabinet that held the intercom speaker. Meantime, he went right on talking.

"Great stuff, brandy. French call it *eau de vie*, and that, in case you don't know it, means 'water of life.' You want a little, eh, ol' buddy? Sure you do." By this time, he'd come back with the bottle and a pair of glasses and was pouring a good dose into each one. "On the other hand, the Irish gave us our name for whisky. Comes from *uisgebeatha*, and by some bloody peculiar coincidence, that also means 'water of life.' So you just set yourself right down here and get some life into you."

Mike sat down at the computer table, and Jeffers sat down across from him. "Now you just drink on up, buddy-buddy, and then tell your ol' Uncle Pete what the bloody hell the trouble is."

Mike looked at the brandy for a full half minute. Then, with one quick flip of his wrist and a sudden spasmodic movement of his gullet, he downed it.

Then he took a deep breath and said: "Do I look as bad as all that?"

"Worse," said Jeffers complacently, meanwhile

133

refilling Mike's glass. "While we were on active service together, I've seen you go through all kinds of things and never look like this. What is it? Reaction from this afternoon's—or, pardon my—*yesterday* afternoon's emergency?"

Mike glanced up at the chronometer. It was two-thirty in the morning, Greenwich time. Jeffers held the bridge from midnight till noon, while Black Bart had the noon to midnight shift.

Still, Mike hadn't realized that it was as late as all that.

He looked at Jeffers' lean, bony face. "Reaction? No, it's not that. Look, Pete, you know me. Would you say I was a pretty levelheaded guy?"

"Sure."

"My old man always said, 'Never make an enemy accidentally,' and I think he was right. So I usually think over what I say before I open my big mouth, don't I?"

Again Jeffers said, "Sure."

"I wouldn't call myself over-cautious," Mike persisted, "but I usually think a thing through pretty carefully before I act—that is, if I have time. Right?"

"I'd say so," Jeffers admitted. "I'd say you were about the only guy I know who does the right thing more than 90 per cent of the time. And says the right thing more than 99 per cent of the time. So what do you want? Back-patting, or just hero worship?"

Mike took a small taste of the brandy. "Neither, you jerk. But about eight hours ago I said something that I hadn't planned to say. I practically proposed to Leda Crannon without knowing I was going to."

Peter Jeffers didn't laugh. He simply said, "How'd it happen?"

134

Mike told him.

When Mike had finished, one drink later, Peter Jeffers filled the glasses for the third time and leaned back in his chair. "Tell me one thing, ol' buddy, and think about it before you answer. If you had a chance to get out of it gracefully, would you take back what you said?"

Mike the Angel thought it over. The sweep hand on the chronometer made its rounds several times before he answered. Then, at last, he said: "No, No, I wouldn't."

Jeffers pursed his lips, then said judicially: "In that case, you're not doing badly at all. There's nothing wrong with you except the fact that you're in love."

Mike downed the third drink fast and stood up. "Thanks, Pete," he said. "That's what I was afraid of."

"Wait just one stinkin' minute," said Jeffers firmly. "Sit down."

Mike sat.

"What do you intend to do about it?" Jeffers asked.

Mike the Angel grinned at him. "What the hell else can I do but woo and win the wench?"

Jeffers grinned back at him. "I reckon you know you got competition, huh?"

"You mean Jake von Liegnitz?" Mike's face darkened. "I have the feeling he's looking for something that doesn't include a marriage certificate."

"Love sure makes a man sound noble," said Jeffers philosophically. "If you mean that all he wants is to get Leda into the sack, you're prob'ly right. Normal reaction, I'd say. Can't blame Jake for that."

"I don't," said Mike. "But that doesn't mean I can't spike his guns."

"Course not. Again, a normal reaction."

"What about Lew Mellon?" Mike asked.

"Lew?" Jeffers raised his eyebrows. "I dunno. I think he likes to talk to her, is all. But if he *is* interested, he's bloody well serious. He's a strict Anglo-Catholic, like yourself."

I'm not as strict at I ought to be, Mike thought. "I thought he had a rather monkish air about him," he said aloud.

Jeffers chuckled. "Yeah, but I don't think he's so ascetic that he wouldn't marry." His grin broadened. "Now, if we were still at ol' Chilblains, you'd *really* have competition. After all, you can't expect that a gal who's stacked . . . pardon me . . . who has the magnificent physical and physiognomical topography of Leda Crannon to spend her life bein' ignored, now can you?"

"Nope," said Mike the Angel.

"Now, I figger," Jeffers said, "that you can purty much forget about Lew Mellon. But Jakob von Liegnitz is a chromatically variant equine, indeed."

Mike shook his head vigorously, as if to clear away the fog. "*Pfui!* Let's change the subject. My heretofore nimble mind has been coagulated by a pair of innocent blue eyes. I need my skull stirred up."

"I have a limerick," said Jeffers lightly. "It's about a young spaceman named Mike, who said: 'I can do as I like!' And to prove his bright quip, he took a round trip, clear to Sirius B on a bike. Or, the tale of the pirate, Black Bart, whose head was as hard as his heart. When he found—"

"Enough!" Mike the Angel held up a hand. "That distillate of fine old grape has made us both silly. Good night. I'm going to get some sleep." He stood up and winked at Jeffers. "And thanks for listening while I bent your ear."

"Any time at all, ol' amoeba. And if you ever feel you need some advice from an ol' married man, why you just trot right round, and I'll give you plenty of bad advice."

"At least you're honest," Mike said. "Night."

Mike the Angel left the bridge as Commander Jeffers was putting the brandy back in its hiding place.

Mike went to his quarters, hit the sack, and spent less than five minutes getting to sleep. There was nothing worrying him now.

He didn't know how long he'd been asleep when he heard a noise in the darkness of his room that made him sit up in bed, instantly awake. The floater under him churned a little, but there was no noise. The room was silent.

In the utter blackness of the room, Mike the Angel could see nothing, and he could hear nothing but the all-pervading hum of the ship's engines. But he could still feel and smell.

He searched back in his memory, trying to place the sound that had awakened him. It hadn't been loud, merely unusual. It had been a noise that shouldn't have been made in the stateroom. It had been a quiet sound, really, but for the life of him, Mike couldn't remember what it had sounded like.

But the evidence of his nerves told him there was someone else in the room besides himself. Somewhere near him, something was radiating heat; it was definitely perceptible in the air-conditioned coolness of his room. And, too, there was the definite smell of warm oil—machine oil. It was faint, but it was unmistakable.

And then he knew what the noise had been.

The soft purr of caterpillar treads against the floor!

Casually, Mike the Angel moved his hand to the wall plaque and touched it lightly. The lights came on, dim and subdued.

"Hello, Snookums," said Mike the Angel gently. "What are you here for?"

The little robot just stood there for a second or two, unmoving, his waldo hands clasped firmly in front of his chest. Mike suddenly wished to Heaven that the metallic face could show something that Mike could read.

"I came for data," said Snookums at last, in the contralto voice that so resembled the voice of the woman who had trained him.

Mike started to say, "At this time of night?" Then he glanced at his wrist. It was after seven-thirty in the morning, Greenwich time—which was also ship time.

"What is it you want?" Mike asked.

"Can you dance?" asked Snookums.

"Yes," said Mike dazedly, "I can dance." For a moment he had the wild idea that Snookums was going to ask him to do a few turns about the floor.

"Thank you," said Snookums. His treads whirred, he turned as though on a pivot, whizzed to the door, opened it, and was gone.

Mike the Angel stared at the door as though trying to see beyond it, into the depths of the robot's brain itself.

"Now just what was *that* all about?" he asked aloud.

In the padded silence of the stateroom, there wasn't even an echo to answer him.

14

Mike the Angel spent the next three days in a pale blue funk which he struggled valiantly against, at least to prevent it from becoming a deep blue.

There was something wrong aboard the *Brainchild*, and Mike simply couldn't quite figure what it was. He found that he wasn't the only one who had been asked peculiar questions by Snookums. The little robot seemed to have developed a sudden penchant for asking seemingly inane questions.

Lieutenant Keku reported with a grin that Snookums had asked him if he knew who Commander Gabriel *really* was.

"What'd you say?" Mike had asked.

Keku had spread his hands and said: "I gave him the usual formula about not being positive of my data, then I told him that you were known as Mike the Angel and were well known in the power field."

Multhaus reported that Snookums had wanted to know what their destination was. The chief's only possible answer, of course, had been: "I don't have that data, Snookums."

Dr. Morris Fitzhugh had become more worried-looking than usual and had confided to Mike that he, too, wondered why Snookums was asking such peculiar questions.

"All he'll tell me," the roboticist had reported, wrinkling up his face, "was that he was collecting data. But he flatly refused, even when ordered, to tell me what he needed the data for."

Mike stayed away from Leda Crannon as much as possible; shipboard was no place to try to conduct a romance. Not that he deliberately avoided her in such a manner as to give offense, but he tried to appear busy at all times.

She was busy, too. Keeping herd on Snookums was becoming something of a problem. She had never attempted to watch him all the time. In the first place, it was physically impossible; in the second place, she didn't think Snookums would develop properly if he were to be kept under constant supervision. But now, for the first time, she didn't have the foggiest notion of what was going on inside the robot's mind, and she couldn't find out. It puzzled and worried her, and between herself and Dr. Fitzhugh there were several long conferences on Snookums' peculiar behavior.

Mike the Angel found himself waiting for something to happen. He hadn't the slightest notion what it was that he was waiting for, but he was as certain of its coming as he was of the fact that the Earth was an oblate spheroid.

But he certainly didn't expect it to begin the way it did.

A quiet evening bridge game is hardly the place for a riot to start.

Pete Jeffers was pounding the pillow in his stateroom; Captain Quill was on the bridge, checking through the log.

In the officers' wardroom Mike the Angel was looking down at two hands of cards, wondering whether he'd make his contract. His own hand held the ace, nine, seven of spades; the ten, six, two of hearts; the jack, ten, nine, four, three, and deuce of diamonds; and the eight of clubs.

Vaneski, his partner, had bid a club. Keku had answered with a take-out double. Mike had looked at his hand, figured that since he and Vaneski were vulnerable, while Keku and von Liegnitz were not, he bid a weakness pre-empt of three diamonds. Von Liegnitz passed, and Vaneski had answered back with five diamonds. Keku and Mike had both passed, and von Liegnitz had doubled.

Now Mike was looking at Vaneski's dummy hand. No spades; the ace, queen, five, and four of hearts; the queen, eight, seven, and six of diamonds; and the ace, king, seven, four, and three of clubs.

And von Liegnitz had led the three of hearts.

It didn't look good. His opponents had the ace and king of trumps, and with von Liegnitz' heart lead, it looked as though he might have to try a finesse on the king of hearts. Still, there *might* be another way out.

Mike threw in the ace from dummy. Keku tossed in his seven, and Mike threw in his own deuce. He took the next trick with the ace of clubs from dummy, and the singleton eight in his own hand. The one after that came from dummy, too; it was the king of clubs, and Mike threw in the heart six from his own hand. From dummy, he led the three of clubs. Keku went over it with a jack, but Mike took it with his deuce of diamonds.

He led the seven of spades to get back in dummy so he could use up those clubs. Dummy took the trick with the six of diamonds, and led out with the four of clubs.

Mike figured that Keku must—absolutely *must*—have the king of hearts. Both his take-out double and von Liegnitz' heart lead pointed toward the king in his hand. Now if . . .

Vaneski had moved around behind Mike to watch the play. Not one of them noticed Lieutenant Lew Mellon, the Medical Officer, come into the room.

That is, they knew he had come in, but they had ignored him thereafter. He was such a colorless non-entity that he simply seemed to fade into the background of the walls once he had made his entrance.

Mike had taken seven tricks, and, as he had expected, lost the eighth to von Liegnitz' five of diamonds. When the German led the nine of hearts, Mike knew he had the game. He put in the queen from dummy, Keku tossed in his king triumphantly, and Mike topped it with his lowly four of diamonds.

If, as he suspected, his opponents' ace and king of diamonds were split, he would get them both by losing the next trick and then make a clean sweep of the board.

He threw in his nine of diamonds.

He just happened to glance at von Liegnitz as the navigator dropped his king.

Then he lashed out with one foot, kicking at the leg of von Liegnitz' chair. At the same time, he yelled, "Jake! Duck!"

He was almost too late. Mellon, his face contorted with a mixture of anger and hatred, was standing just behind Jakob von Liegnitz. In one hand was a heavy spanner, which he was bringing down with deadly force on the navigator's skull.

Von Liegnitz' chair started to topple, and von Liegnitz himself spun away from the blow. The spanner caught him on the shoulder, and he grunted in pain, but he kept on moving away from Mellon.

The medic screamed something and lifted the spanner again.

By this time, Keku, too, was on his feet, moving toward Mellon. Mike the Angel got behind Mellon, trying to grab at the heavy metal tool in Mellon's hand.

Mellon seemed to sense him, for he jumped sideways, out of Mike's way, and kicked backward at the same time, catching Mike on the shin with his heel.

Von Liegnitz had made it to his feet by this time and was blocking the downward swing of Mellon's arm with his own forearm. His other fist pistoned out toward Mellon's face. It connected, sending Mellon staggering backward into Mike the Angel's arms.

Von Liegnitz grabbed the spanner out of Mellon's hand and swung it toward the medic's jaw. It was only inches away when Keku's hand grasped the navigator's wrist.

And when the big Hawaiian's hand clamped on, von Liegnitz' hand stopped almost dead.

Mellon was screaming. "You—!" He ran out a string of unprintable and almost un-understandable words. "I'll kill you! I'll do it yet! *You stay away from Leda Crannon!*"

"Calm down, Doc!" snapped Mike the Angel. "What the hell's the matter with you, anyway?"

Von Liegnitz was still straining, trying to get away from Keku to take another swipe at the medic, but the huge Hawaiian held him easily. The navigator had lapsed into his native German, and most of it was unintelligible, except for an occasional reference to various improbable combinations of animal life.

But Mellon was paying no attention. "You! I'll kill you! Lecher! Dirty-minded, filthy . . ."

He went on.

Suddenly, unexpectedly, he smashed his heel down on Mike's toe. At least, he tried to; he'd have done it if the toe had been there when his heel came down. But Mike moved it just two inches and avoided the blow.

At the same time, though, Mellon twisted, and Mike's forced shift of position lessened his leverage on the man's shoulders and arms. Mellon almost got away. One hand grabbed the wrench from von Liegnitz, whose grip had been weakened by the paralyzing pressure of Keku's fingers.

Mike had no choice but to slam a hard left into the man's solar plexus. Mellon collapsed like an unoccupied overcoat.

By this time, von Liegnitz had quieted down. "Let go, Keku," he said. "I'm all right." He looked down at the motionless figure on the deck. "What the hell do you suppose was eating him?" he asked quietly.

"How's your shoulder?" Mike asked.

"Hurts like the devil, but I don't think it's busted. But why did he do it?" he repeated.

"Sounds to me," said Keku dryly, "that he was nutty jealous of you. He didn't like the times you took Leda Crannon to the base movies while we were at Chilblains."

Jakob von Liegnitz continued to look down at the smaller man in wonder. "*Lieber Gott*," he said finally.

144

"I only took her out a couple of times. I knew he liked her, but—" He stopped. "The guy must be off his bearings."

"I smelled liquor on his breath," said Mike. "Let's get him down to his stateroom and lock him in until he sobers up. I'll have to report this to the captain. Can you carry him, Keku?"

Keku nodded and reached down. He put his hands under Mellon's armpits, lifted him to his feet, and threw him over his shoulder.

"Good," said Mike the Angel. "I'll walk behind you and clop him one if he wakes up and gets wise."

Vaneski was standing to one side, his face pale, his expression blank.

Mike said: "Jake, you and Vaneski go up and make the report to the captain. Tell him we'll be up as soon as we've taken care of Mellon."

"Right," said von Liegnitz, massaging his bruised shoulder.

"Okay, Keku," said Mike, "forward march."

Lieutenant Keku thumbed the opener to Mellon's stateroom, shoved the door aside, stepped in, and slapped at the switch plaque. The plates lighted up, bathing the room in sunshiny brightness.

"Dump him on his sack," said Mike.

While Keku put the unconscious Mellon on his bed, Mike let his gaze wander around the room. It was neat—almost too neat, implying overfussiness. The medical reference books were on one shelf, all in alphabetical order. Another shelf contained a copy of the *International Encyclopedia,* English edition, plus several dictionaries, including one on medical terms and another on theological ones.

On the desk lay a copy of the Bible, York translation, opened to the Book of Tobit. Next to it were several sheets of blank paper and a small traveling clock sat on them as a paperweight.

His clothing was hung neatly, in the approved regulation manner, with his shoes in their proper places and his caps all lined up in a row.

Mike walked around the room, looking at everything.

"What's the matter? What're you looking for?" asked Keku.

"His liquor," said Mike the Angel.

"In his desk, lower left-hand drawer. You won't find anything but a bottle of ruby port; Mellon was never a drinker."

Mike opened the drawer. "I probably won't find that, drunk as he is."

Surprisingly enough, the bottle of wine was almost half full. "Did he have more than one bottle?" Mike asked.

"Not so far as I know. Like I said, he didn't drink much. One slug of port before bedtime was about his limit."

Mike frowned. "How does his breath smell to you?"

"Not bad. Two or three drinks, maybe."

"Mmmm." Mike put the bottle on top of the desk, then walked over to the small case that was standing near one wall. He lifted it and flipped it open. It was the standard medical kit for Space Service physicians.

The intercom speaker squeaked once before Captain Quill's voice came over it. "Mister Gabriel?"

"Yes, sir?" said Mike without turning around. There were no eyes in the private quarters of the officers and crew.

"How is Mister Mellon?" A Space Service physician's doctorate is never used as a form of address; three out of four Space Service officers have a doctor's degree of some kind, and there's no point in calling 75 per cent of the officers "doctor."

Mike glanced across the room. Keku had finished stripping the little physician to his underclothes and had put a cover over him.

"He's still unconscious, sir, but his breathing sounds all right."

"How's his pulse?"

Keku picked up Mellon's left wrist and applied his fingers to the artery while he looked at his wrist watch.

Mike said: "We'll check it, sir. Wait a few seconds."

Fifteen seconds later, Keku multiplied by four and said: "One-oh-four and rather weak."

"You'd better get hold of the Physician's Mate," Mike told Quill. "He's not in good condition, either mentally or physically."

"Very well. As soon as the mate takes over, you and Mister Keku get up here. I want to know what the devil has been going on aboard my ship."

"You are bloody well not the only one," said Mike the Angel.

15

Midnight, ship time.

And, as far as the laws of simultaneity would allow, it was midnight in Greenwich, England. At least, when a ship returned from an interstellar trip, the ship's chronometer was within a second or two, plus or minus, of Greenwich time. Theoretically, the molecular vibration clocks shouldn't vary at all. The fact that they did hadn't yet been satisfactorily accounted for.

Mike the Angel tried to make himself think of clocks or the variations in space time or anything else equally dull, in the hope that it would put him to sleep.

He began to try to work out the derivation of the Beale equations, the equations which had solved the principle of the no-space drive. The ship didn't move through space; space moved through the ship, which, of course, might account for the variation in time, because—

—the time is out of joint.

The time is out of joint: O cursed spite,
That ever I was born to set it right!

Hamlet, thought Mike. *Act One, the end of scene five.*

But why had he been born to set it right? Besides, exactly what was wrong? There was something wrong, all right.

And why from the end of the act? Another act to come? Something more to happen? The clock will go round till another time comes. Watch the clock, the absolutely cuckoo clock, which ticked as things happened that made almost no sense and yet had sense hidden in their works.

The good old Keku clock. Somewhere is icumen in, lewdly sing Keku. The Mellon is ripe and climbing Jakob's ladder. And both of them playing Follow the Leda.

And where were they heading? Toward some destination in the general direction of the constellation Cygnus. The transformation equations work fine on an interstellar ship. Would they work on a man? Wouldn't it be nice to be able to transform yourself into a swan? Cygnus the Swan.

And we'll *all* play Follow the Leda . . .

Somewhere in there, Mike the Angel managed to doze off.

He awoke suddenly, and his dream of being a huge black swan vanished, shattered into nothingness.

This time it had not been a sound that had awakened him. It had been something else, something more like a cessation of sound. A dying sigh.

He reached out and touched the switch plaque.

Nothing happened.

The room remained dark.

The room was strangely silent. The almost soundless vibration of the engines was still there, but . . .

The air conditioners!

The air in the stateroom was unmoving, static. There was none of the faint breeze of moving air. Something had gone wrong with the low-power circuits!

Now how the hell could that happen? Not by accident, unless the accident were a big one. It would take a tremendous amount of coincidence to put all three of the interacting systems out of order at once. And they all *had* to go at once to cut the power from the low-load circuits.

The standard tap and the first and second stand-by taps were no longer tapping power from the main generators. The intercom was gone, too, along with the air conditioners, the lights, and half a dozen other sub circuits.

Mike the Angel scrambled out of bed and felt for his clothing, wishing he had something as prosaic as an old-fashioned match, or even a flame-type cigarette lighter. He found his lighter in his belt pocket as he pulled on his uniform. He jerked it out and thumbed it. In the utter darkness, the orange-red glow gave more illumination than he had supposed. If a man's eyes are adjusted to darkness, he can read print by the glow of a cigarette, and the lighter's glow was brighter than that.

Still, it wasn't much. If only he had a flashlight!

From a distance, far down the companionway, he could hear voices. The muffled sound that had awakened him had been the soft susurration of the door as it had slid open when the power died. Without the electrolocks to hold it closed, it had opened automatically. The doors in a spaceship are built that way, to make sure no one will be trapped in case of a power failure.

Mike dressed in a matter of seconds and headed toward the door.

And stopped just before he stepped out.

Someone was outside. Someone, or—something.

He didn't know *how* he knew, but he knew. He was as certain as if the lights had been on bright.

And whoever was waiting out there didn't want Mike the Angel to know that he was there.

Mike stood silent for a full second. That was long enough for him to get angry. Not the hot anger of hatred, but the cold anger of a man who has had too many attempts on his life, who has escaped narrowly from an unseen plotter twice because of pure luck and does not intend to fall victim to the dictum that "the third time's a charm."

He realized that he was still holding the glowing cigarette lighter in his hand.

"Damn!" he muttered, as though to himself. "I'd forget my ears if they weren't sewed down." Then he turned, heading back toward his bed, hoping that whoever was waiting outside would assume he would be back immediately. At the same time, he lifted his thumb off the lighter's contact.

Then he sat down on the edge of his bed and quickly pulled off his boots. Holding them both in his hands, he moved silently back to the door. When he reached it, he tossed both boots to the rear of the room. When they landed clatteringly, he stepped quietly through the door. In three steps he was on the opposite side of the corridor. He hugged the wall and moved back away from the spot where the watcher would be expecting him.

152

Then he waited.

He was on one side of the door to his stateroom, and the—what or whoever it was—was on the other. Until that other made a move, Mike the Angel would wait.

The wait seemed many minutes long, although Mike knew it couldn't have been more than forty-five seconds or so. From other parts of the ship he could hear voices shouting as the crewmen and officers who had been sleeping were awakened by the men on duty. The ship could not sustain life long if the air conditioners were dead.

Then, quite suddenly, the waiting was over. Behind Mike there was a bend in the corridor, and from around that bend came the sound of running footsteps, followed by a bellowing voice: "I'll get the Commander; you go down and get the other boys started!"

Multhaus.

And then there was a glow of light. The Chief Powerman's Mate was carrying a light, which reflected from the walls of the corridor.

And Mike the Angel knew perfectly well that he was silhouetted against that glow. Whoever it was who was waiting for him could see him plainly.

Multhaus' footsteps rang in the corridor while Mike strained his eyes to see what was before him in the darkness. And all the time, the glow became brighter as Multhaus approached.

Then, from out of the darkness, came something that moved on a whir of caterpillar treads. Something hard and metallic slammed against Mike's shoulder, spinning him against the wall.

At that moment, Multhaus came around the corner, and Mike could see Snookums scurrying on down the corridor toward the approaching Powerman's Mate.

"Multhaus! Look out!" Mike yelled.

The beam from the chief's hand torch gleamed on the metallic body of the little robot as it headed toward him.

"Snookums! Stop!" Mike ordered.

Snookums paid no attention. He swerved adroitly around the astonished Multhaus, spun around the corner, and was gone into the darkness.

"What was all that, sir?" Multhaus asked, looking more than somewhat confused.

"A course of instruction on the First and Second Laws of Robotics as applied by the Computer Corporation of Earth," said Mike, rubbing his bruised side. "But never mind that now. What's wrong with the low-power circuits?"

"I don't know, sir. Breckwell is on duty in that section."

"Let's go," said Mike the Angel. "We have to get this cleared up before we all suffocate."

"Someone's going to get galloping claustrophobia before it's over, anyway," said Multhaus morosely as he followed Mike down the hallway in the direction from which Snookums had come. "Darkness and stuffy air touch off that sort of thing."

"Who's Officer of the Watch tonight?" Mike wanted to know.

"Ensign Vaneski, I think. His name was on the roster, as I remember."

"I hope he reported to the bridge. Commander Jeffers will be getting frantic, but he can't leave the bridge unless he's relieved. Come on, let's move."

They sprinted down the companionway.

The lights had been out less than five minutes when

154

Mike the Angel and Chief Powerman's Mate Multhaus reached the low-power center of the Power Section. The door was open, and a torch was spearing its beam on two men—one kneeling over the prone figure of the other. The kneeling man jerked his head around as Mike and the chief came in the door.

The kneeling man was Powerman First Class Fleck. Mike recognized the man on the floor as Powerman Third Class Breckwell.

"What happened?" he snapped at Fleck.

"Don't know, sir. I was in the head when the lights went. It took me a little time to get a torch and get in here, and I found Breckwell gone. At least, I thought he was gone, but then I heard a noise from the tool cabinet and I opened it and he fell out." The words seemed to come out all in a rush.

"Dead?" asked Mike sharply.

"Nossir, I don't think so, sir. Looks like somebody clonked him on the head, but he's breathin' all right."

Mike knelt over the man and took his pulse. The heartbeat was regular and steady, if a trifle weak. Mike ran a hand over Breckwell's head.

"There's a knot there the size of a golf ball, but I don't think anything's broken," he said.

Footsteps came running down the hall, and six men of the power crew came pouring in the door. They slowed to a halt when they saw their commanding officer was already there.

"A couple of you take care of Breckwell—Leister, Knox—move him to one side. Bathe his face with water. No, wait; you can't do that till we get the pumps moving again. Just watch him."

One of the men coughed a little. "What he needs is a

good slug of hooch.''

"I agree," said Mike evenly. "Too bad there isn't any aboard. But do what you think is best; I'm going to be too busy to keep an eye on you. I won't be able to watch you at all, so you'll be on your own."

"Yessir," said the man who had spoken. He hid his grin and took out at a run, heading for wherever it was he kept his bottle hidden.

"Dunstan, you and Ghihara get out and watch the halls. If any other officer comes this way, sing out."

"Yessir!" came the twin chorus.

More footsteps pounded toward them, and the remaining men of the power crew arrived.

"All right, now let's take a look at these circuits," said Mike.

Chief Multhaus had already flipped open all the panels and was peering inside. The men lined the torches up on the desk in the corner, in order to shed as much light as possible over the banks of low-power wiring, and went over to where Multhaus and Mike the Angel were standing.

"Dig out three replacement switches—heavy-duty six-double-oh-B-nines," said Multhaus. There was a touch of disgust and a good-sized serving of anger and irritation in his voice.

Mike the Angel surveyed the damage. "See anything else, Multhaus?"

"No, sir. That's it."

Mike nodded. "About five minutes' work to get the main switch going, which will give us power, and another ten minutes for the first and second stand-bys. Go ahead and take over, Multhaus; you won't need me. I'll go find out what the bloody unprintable is going on around here."

Mike the Angel ran into Captain Sir Henry Quill as he went up the companionway to the bridge.

"What happened?" demanded the captain in his gravelly tenor voice.

"Somebody ripped out the main switches to the low-power taps from the main generators, sir," said Mike. "Nothing to worry about. The boys will have the lights on within three or four minutes."

"Who . . . ?"

"I don't know," said Mike, "but we'd better find out pretty fast. There've been too many things going on aboard this ship to suit me."

"Same here. Are you sure everything's all right down there?"

"Absolutely, sir. We can quit worrying about the damage itself and put our minds to finding out who did that damage."

"Do you have any ideas?"

"Some," said Mike the Angel. "As soon as the intercom is functioning again, I think you'd better call a general meeting of officers—and get Miss Crannon and Fitzhugh out of bed and get them up here, too."

"Why?" Black Bart asked flatly.

"Because Snookums has gone off his rocker. He's attacked at least one human being that I know of and has ignored direct orders from a human being."

"Who?" asked Black Bart.

"Me," said Mike the Angel.

Mike told Captain Quill what had happened as they made their way back up to the bridge.

Ensign Vaneski, looking pale and worried, met them at the door. He snapped a salute. "I just reported to Commander Jeffers, sir. Something's wrong with the low-power circuits."

"I had surmised as much," said Black Bart caustically. "Anything new? What did you find out? What happened?"

"When the lights went out, I was having coffee by myself in the wardroom. I grabbed a torch and headed for Power Section as soon as I could. The low-power room was empty. There should have been a man on duty there, but there wasn't. I didn't want to go inside, since I'm not a power officer, so I came up here to report. I—"

At that moment the lights blazed on again. There was a faint hum that built up all over the ship as the air conditioning came on at the same time.

"All right, Mister Vaneski," said Black Bart, "get below and take care of things. There's a man hurt down there, so be ready to take him to sick bay when the Physician's Mate gets there. We don't have a medic in any condition to take care of people, so he'll have to do. Hop it."

As Vaneski left, Black Bart preceded Mike into the bridge. Pete Jeffers was on the intercom. As Mike and the captain came in, he was saying, "All right. I'll notify the Officer of the Watch, and we'll search the ship. He can't hide very long." Then, without waiting to say anything to Mike or Quill, he jabbed at another button. "Mister von Liegnitz! Jake!"

"*Ja*? Huh? What is it?" came a fuzzy voice from the speaker.

"You all right?"

"Me? Sure. I was asleep. Why?"

"Be on your toes, sleepyhead; just got word that Mellon has escaped from his stateroom. He may try to take another crack at you."

158

"I'll watch it," said von Liegnitz, his voice crisp now.

"Okay." Jeffers sighed and looked up. "As soon as the power came on, the Physician's Mate was on the intercom. Mellon isn't in his stateroom."

"Oh, wonderful!" growled Captain Quill. "We now have one insane robot and one insane human running loose on this ship. I'm glad we didn't bring any gorillas with us."

"Somehow I think I'd be safer with a gorilla," said Mike the Angel.

"According to the Physician's Mate, Mellon is worse than just nuts," said Jeffers quietly. "He says he loaded Mellon full of dope to make him sleep and that the man's got no right to be walkin' around at all."

"He must have gotten out while the doors were open," said Captain Quill. He rubbed the palm of his hand over the shiny pinkness of his scalp. His dark, shaggy brows were down over his eyes, as though they had been weighted with lead.

"Mister Jeffers," he said abruptly, "break out the stun guns. Issue one to each officer and one to each chief noncom. Until we get this straightened out, I'm declaring a state of emergency."

16

Mike the Angel hefted the heavy stun gun in his right fist, feeling its weight without really noticing it. He knew damned good and well it wouldn't be of any use against Snookums. If Mellon came at him, the supersonic beam from the gun would affect his nerves the same way an electric current would, and he'd collapse, unconscious but relatively unharmed. But Mike doubted seriously that it would have any effect at all on the metal body of the robot. It is as difficult to jolt the nerves of a robot as it is to blind an oyster.

Snookums did have sensory devices that enabled him to tell what was going on around him, but they were not nerves in the ordinary sense of the word, and a stun gun certainly wouldn't have the same effect.

He wondered just what effect it *would* have—if any.

He was going down the main ladder—actually a long spiral stairway that led downward from the bridge. Behind him were Chief Multhaus, also armed with a stun gun, and four members of the power crew, each armed with a heavy spanner. Mike or the chief could take care of Mellon; it would be the crew's job to take care of Snookums.

"Smash his treads and his waldoes," Mike had told them, "but only if he attacks. Before you try anything else, give him an order to halt. If he keeps on coming, start swinging." And, to Chief Multhaus: "If Mellon jumps me, fire that stun gun only if he's armed with a knife or a gun. But if you do have to fire at Mellon, don't wait to get in a good shot; just go ahead and knock us both out. I'd rather be asleep than dead. Okay?"

Multhaus had agreed. "The same goes for me, Commander. And the rest of the boys."

So down the ladder they went. Mike hoped there'd be no fighting at all. He had the feeling that everything was all wrong, somehow, and that any use of stun guns or spanners would just make everything worse.

His wasn't the only group looking for Snookums and Mellon. Lieutenant Keku had another group, and Commander Jeffers had a third. Lieutenant Commander von Liegnitz was with Captain Quill on the bridge. Mellon had already attacked von Liegnitz once; the captain didn't want them mixing it up again.

Captain Quill's voice came suddenly from a speaker in the overhead. "Miss Crannon and Dr. Fitzhugh have just spoken to me," he said in his brisk tenor. "Snookums is safe in his own room. I have outlined what has happened, and they're trying to get information from Snookums now. Lieutenant Mellon is still missing."

"One down," said Chief Multhaus. There was relief in his voice.

"Let's see if we can find the other one," said Mike the Angel.

They went down perhaps three more steps, and the speakers came to life again. "Will the Chief Physician's Mate report to Commander Jeffers in the maintenance tool room? Lieutenant Keku, dismiss your men to quarters and report to the bridge. Commander Gabriel, dismiss your men to quarters and report to Commander Jeffers in maintenance. All chief non-coms report to the ordnance room to turn in your weapons. All enlisted men return to your posts or to quarters."

Mike the Angel holstered his stun gun. "That's two down," he said to Chief Multhaus.

"Looks like we missed all the fun," said Multhaus.

"Okay, men," Mike said, "you got the word. Take those spanners back to the tool room in Power Section, and then get back to your quarters. Chief, you go with them and secure everything, then take that stun gun back to ordnance."

"Yessir."

Multhaus threw Mike a salute; Mike returned it and headed toward maintenance. He knew Multhaus and the others were curious, but he was just as curious himself. He had the advantage of being in a position to satisfy his curiosity.

The maintenance tool room was big and lined with tool lockers. One of them was open. Sprawled in front of it was Lieutenant Mellon. Over to one side was Commander Jeffers, standing next to a white-faced Ensign Vaneski. Nearby were a chief non-com and three enlisted men.

"Hullo, Mike," Pete Jeffers said as Mike the Angel came in.

"What happened, Pete?" Mike asked.

Jeffers gestured at the sprawled figure on the floor. "We came in here to search. We found him. Mister

163

Vaneski opened the locker, there, for a look-see, and Mellon jumped out at him. Vaneski fired his stun gun. Mellon collapsed to the deck. He's in bad shape; his pulse is so weak that it's hard to find.''

Mike the Angel walked over and looked down at the fallen Medical Officer. His face was waxen, and he looked utterly small and harmless.

"What happened?" asked another voice from the door. It was Chief Physician's Mate Pierre Pasteur. He was a smallish man, well rounded, pleasant-faced, and inordinately proud of his name. He couldn't actually prove that he was really descended from the great Louis, but he didn't allow people to think otherwise. Like most C. Phys. M.'s, he had a doctor of medicine degree but no internship in the Space Service. He was working toward his commission.

"We've got a patient for you," said Jeffers. "Better look him over, Chief."

Chief Pasteur walked over to where Mellon lay and took his stethoscope out of his little black bag. He listened to Mellon's chest for a few seconds. Then he pried open an eyelid and looked closely at an eye. "What happened to him?" he asked, without looking up.

"Got hit with a beam from a stun gun," said Jeffers.

"How did he fall? Did he hit his head?"

"I don't know—maybe." He looked at Ensign Vaneski. "Did he, Mister Vaneski? He was right on top of you; I was across the room."

Vaneski swallowed. "I don't know. He—he just sort of—well, he *fell*."

"You didn't catch him?" asked the chief. He was a physician on a case now and had no time for sirring his

164

superiors.

"No. No. I jumped away from him."

"Why? What's the trouble?" Jeffers asked.

"He's dead," said the Chief Physician's Mate.

17

Leda Crannon was standing outside the cubicle that had been built for Snookums. Her back and the palms of her hands were pressed against the door. Her head was bowed, and her red hair, shining like a hellish flame in the light of the glow panels, fell around her shoulders and cheeks, almost covering her face.

"Leda," said Mike the Angel gently.

She looked up. There were tears in her blue eyes.

"Mike! Oh, Mike!" She ran toward him, put her arms around him, and tried to bury her face in Mike's chest.

"What's the matter, honey? What's happened?" He was certain she couldn't have heard about Mellon's death yet. He held her in his arms, carefully, tenderly, not passionately.

"He's crazy, Mike. He's completely crazy." Her voice had suddenly lost everything that gave it color. It was only dead and choked.

Mike the Angel knew it was an emotional reaction. As a psychologist, she would never have used the word "crazy." But as a woman . . . as a human being . . .

"Fitz is still in there talking to him, but he's—he's—" Her voice choked off again into sobs.

Mike waited patiently, holding her, caressing her hair.

"Eight years," she said after a minute or so. "Eight years I spent. And now he's gone. He's broken."

"How do you know?" Mike asked.

She lifted her head and looked at him. "Mike—did he really hit you? Did he refuse to stop when you ordered him to? What *really* happened?"

Mike told her what had happened in the darkened companionway just outside his room.

When he finished, she began sobbing again. "He's lying, Mike," she said. "*Lying!*"

Mike nodded silently and slowly. Leda Crannon had spent all of her adult life tending the hurts and bruises and aches of Snookums the Child. She had educated him, cared for him, taken pleasure in his triumphs, worried about his health, and watched him grow mentally.

And now he was sick, broken, ruined. And, like all parents, she was asking herself: "What did *I* do wrong?"

Mike the Angel didn't give her an answer to that unspoken question, but he knew what the answer was in so many cases:

The grieving parent has not necessarily done anything wrong. It may simply be that there was insufficient or poor-quality material to work with.

With a human child, it is even more humiliating for a parent to admit that he or she has contributed inferior genetic material to a child than it is to admit a failure in upbringing. Leda's case was different.

Leda had lost her child, but Mike hesitated to point out that it wasn't her fault in the first place because the material wasn't up to the task she had given it, and in the second place because she hadn't really lost anything. She was still playing with dolls, not human beings.

"Hell!" said Mike under his breath, not realizing that he was practically whispering in her ear.

"Isn't it?" she said. "Isn't it Hell? I spent eight years trying to make that little mind of his tick properly. I wanted to know what was the right, proper, and logical way to bring up children. I had a theory, and I wanted to test it. And now I'll never know."

"What sort of theory?" Mike asked.

She sniffled, took a handkerchief from her pocket, and began wiping at her tears. Mike took the handkerchief away from her and did the wiping job himself. "What's this theory?" he said.

"Oh, it isn't important now. But I felt—I still feel—that everybody is born with a sort of Three Laws of Robotics in him. You know what I mean—that a person wouldn't kill or harm anyone, or refuse to do what was right, in addition to trying to preserve his own life. I think babies are born that way. But I think that the information they're given when they're growing up can warp them. They still think they're obeying the laws, but they're obeying them wrongly, if you see what I mean."

Mike nodded without saying anything. This was no time to interrupt her.

"For instance," she went on, "if my theory's right, then a child would never disobey his father—unless he was convinced that the man was not really his father, you see. For instance, if he learned, very early, that his father never spanks him, that becomes one of the identifying marks of 'father.' Fine. But the first time his father *does* spank him, doubt enters. If that sort of thing goes on, he becomes disobedient because he doesn't believe that the man is his father.

"I'm afraid I'm putting it a little crudely, but you get the idea."

"Yeah," said Mike. For all he knew, there might be some merit in the girl's idea; he knew that philosophers had talked of the "basic goodness of mankind" for centuries. But he had a hunch that Leda was going about it wrong. Still, this was no time to argue with her. She seemed calmer now, and he didn't want to upset her any more than he had to.

"That's what you've been working on with Snookums?" he asked.

"That's it."

"For eight years?"

"For eight years."

"Is that the information, the data, that makes Snookums so priceless, aside from his nucleonics work?"

She smiled a little then. "Oh no. Of course not, silly. He's been fed data on everything—physics, subphysics, chemistry, mathematics—all kinds of things. Most of the major research laboratories on Earth have problems of one kind or another that Snookums has been working on. He hasn't been given the problem *I* was working on at all; it would bias him." Then the tears came back. "And now it doesn't matter. He's insane. He's lying."

"What's he saying?"

"He insists that he's never broken the First Law, that he has never hurt a human being. And he insists that he has followed the orders of human beings, according to the Second Law."

"May I talk to him?" Mike asked.

She shook her head. "Fitz is running him through an analysis. He even made me leave." Then she looked at his face more closely. "You don't just want to confront him and call him a liar, do you? No—that's not like you. You know he's just a machine—better than I do, I guess . . . What is it, Mike?"

No, he thought, looking at her, *she still thinks he's human. Otherwise, she'd know that a computer can't lie—not in the human sense of the word.*

Most people, if told that a man had said one thing, and that a computer had given a different answer, would rely on the computer.

"What is it, Mike?" she repeated.

"Lew Mellon," he said very quietly, "is dead."

The blood drained from her face, leaving her skin stark against the bright red of her hair. For a moment he thought she was going to faint. Then a little of the color came back.

"Snookums." Her voice was whispery.

He shook his head. "No. Apparently he tried to jump Vaneski and got hit with a stun beam. It shouldn't have killed him—but apparently it did."

"God, God, God," she said softly. "Here I've been crying about a damned machine, and poor Lew has been lying up there dead." She buried her face in her hands, and her voice was muffled when she spoke again. "And I'm all cried out, Mike. I can't cry any more."

Before Mike could make up his mind whether to say anything or not, the door of Snookums' room opened and Dr. Fitzhugh came out, closing the door behind him. There was an odd, stricken look on his face. He looked at Leda and then at Mike, but the expression on his face showed that he really hadn't seen them clearly.

171

"Did you ever wonder if a robot had a soul, Mike?" he asked in a wondering tone.

"No," Mike admitted.

Leda took her hands from her face and looked at him. Her expression was a bright blank stare.

"He won't answer my questions," Fitzhugh said in a hushed tone. "I can't complete the analysis."

"What's that got to do with his soul?" Mike asked.

"He won't answer my questions," Fitzhugh repeated, looking earnestly at Mike. "He says God won't allow him to."

18

Captain Sir Henry Quill opened the door of the late Lieutenant Mellon's quarters and went in, followed by Mike the Angel. The dead man's gear had to be packed away so that it could be given to his nearest of kin when the officers and crew of the *Brainchild* returned to Earth. Regulations provided that two officers must inventory his personal effects and those belonging to the Space Service.

"Does Chief Pasteur know what killed him yet, Captain?" Mike asked.

Quill shook his head. "No. He wants my permission to perform an autopsy."

"Are you going to let him?"

"I think not. We'll put the body in the freezer and have the autopsy performed on Earth." He looked around the room, seeing it for the first time.

"If you don't," said Mike, "you've got three suspected killers on your hands."

Quill was unperturbed. "Don't be ridiculous, Golden Wings."

"I'm not," Mike said. "I hit him in the pit of his stomach. Chief Pasteur filled him full of sedative. Mister Vaneski shot him with a stun beam. He died. Which one of us did it?"

"Probably no single one of them, but a combination of all three," said Captain Quill. "Each action was performed in the line of duty and without malice aforethought—without even intent to harm permanently, much less to kill. There will have to be a court-martial, of course—or, at the very least, a board of inquiry will be appointed. But I am certain you'll all come through any such inquiry scatheless." He picked up a book from Mellon's desk. "Let's get about our business, Mister Gabriel. Mark down: Bible, one."

Mike put it down on the list.

"*International Encyclopedia*, English edition. Thirty volumes and index."

Mike put it down.

"*The Oxford-Webster Dictionary of the English Language—*

"*Hallbert's Dictionary of Medical Terms—*

"*The Canterbury Theological Dictionary—*

"*The Christian Religion and Symbolic Logic,* by Bishop K.F. Costin—

"*The Handbook of Space Medicine—*"

As Captain Quill called out the names of the books and put them into the packing case he'd brought, Mike marked them down—while something began ticking in the back of his mind.

"Item," said Captain Quill, "one crucifix." He paused. "Beautifully carved, too." He put it into the packing case.

"Excuse me, Captain," said Mike suddenly. "Let me

take a look at something, will you?" Excitedly, he leaned over and took some of the books out, looking at the pages of each one.

"I'll be damned," he said after a moment. "Or I *should* be—for being such a stupid idiot!"

Captain Quill narrowed his eyes. "What are you talking about, Mister Gabriel?"

"I'm not sure yet, Captain," Mike hedged. "May I borrow these three books?" He held them up in his hands.

"May I be so bold as to ask *why*, Mister Gabriel?"

"I just want to look at them, sir," Mike said. "I'll return them within a few hours."

"Mister Gabriel," Captain Quill said, "after what happened last night, I am suspicious of everything that goes on aboard this ship. But—yes. You may take them. However, I want them returned before we land tomorrow morning."

Mike blinked. Neither he nor anyone else—with the exception of Captain Quill and Lieutenant Commander von Liegnitz, the navigator, knew the destination of the ship. Mike hadn't realized they were that close to their goal. "I'll have them back by then," he promised.

"Very well. Now let's get on about our work."

The job was completed within forty-five minutes. A man can't carry a great deal with him on a spaceship. When they were through, Mike the Angel excused himself and went to his quarters. Two hours after that he went to the officers' wardroom to look up Pete Jeffers. Pete hadn't been in his quarters, and Mike knew he wasn't on duty by that time. Sure enough, Jeffers was drinking coffee all by himself in the wardroom. He looked up when Mike came in.

"Hullo, Mike," he said listlessly. "Come sit. Have some coffee."

There was a faint aroma in the air which indicated that there was more in the cup than just coffee. "No, thanks, Pete. I'll sit this one out. I wanted to talk to you."

"Sit. I am drinking a toast to Mister Lew Mellon." He pointed at the coffee. "Sure you won't have a mite? It's sweetened from the grape."

"No, thanks again." Mike sat down. "It's Mellon I wanted to talk about. Did you know him well, Pete?"

"Purty well," Pete said, nodding. "Yeah, purty well. I always figured him for a great little bloke. Can't figure what got into him."

"Me either. Pete, you told me he was an Anglo-Catholic—a good one, you said."

" 'At's right."

"Well, how did you mean that?"

Pete frowned. "Just what I said. He studied his religion, he went to Mass regularly, said his prayers—that sort of thing. And he was, I will say, a Christian gentleman in every sense of the word." There was irritation in his voice, as though Mike had impugned the memory of a friend.

"Don't get huffy, Pete; he struck me as a pretty nice person, too—"

"Until he flipped his lid," said Pete. "But that might happen to anybody."

"Sure. But what I want to know—and don't get sore—is, did he show any kind of—well, *instability* before this last outbreak?"

"Like what?"

"I mean, was he a religious nut? Did he act 'holier

176

than thou' or—well, was he a fanatic, would you say?''

"No, I wouldn't say so. He didn't talk much about it. I guess you noticed that. I mean, he didn't preach. He smoked some and had his glass of wine now and then—even had a cocktail or two on occasion. His views on sex were orthodox, I reckon—I mean, as far as I know. He'd tell an off-color story, if it wasn't *too* bad. But he'd get up and leave quietly if the boys started tellin' about the women they'd made. Fornication and adultery just weren't his meat, I'd say.''

"I know he wasn't married,'' Mike said. "Did he date much?''

"Some. He liked to dance. Women seemed to like him.''

"How about men?''

"Most of the boys liked him.''

"That's not what I meant.''

"Oh. Was he queer?'' Pete frowned. "I'd damn near stake my life that he wasn't.''

"You mean he didn't practice it?''

"I don't believe he even thought about it,'' Pete said. "Course, you can't tell what's really goin' on in a man's mind, but—'' His frown became a scowl. "Damn it, Mike, just because a man isn't married by the time he's thirty-five and practices Christian chastity, while he's single don't necessarily mean he's a damn fairy!''

"I didn't say it did. I just wondered if you'd heard anything.''

"No more'n I've heard about you—who are in exactly the same position!''

"Exactly,'' Mike agreed. "That's what I wanted to know. Pete, if you've got it to spare, I'll join you in that toast.''

177

Pete Jeffers grinned. "Comin' right up, buddy-boy."

He poured two more cups of coffee, spiked them from a small flask of brandy, and handed one to Mike. They drank in silence.

Fifteen minutes later, Mike the Angel was in the little office that Leda Crannon shared with Dr. Fitzhugh. She was alone.

"How's the girl today?" he asked.

"Beat," she said with a forced smile.

"You look beautiful," he said. He wasn't lying. She looked drawn and tired, but she still looked beautiful.

"Thanks, Mike. What can I do for you?"

Mike the Angel pulled up a chair and sat down. "Where's Doc Fitz?"

"He's still trying to get information out of Snookums. It's a weird thing, Mike—a robot with a soul."

"You don't mind talking about it?"

"No; go ahead if you want."

"All right, answer me a question," he said. "Can Snookums read English?"

"Certainly. And Russian, and German, French, Chinese, and most of the other major languages of Earth."

"He could read a book, then?"

"Yes. But not unless it was given to him and he was specifically told to use its contents as data."

"Good," said Mike. "Now, suppose Snookums was given complete data on a certain field of knowledge. Suppose further that this field is internally completely logical, completely coherent, completely self-consistent. Suppose it could even be reduced to a series of axioms and theorems in symbolic logic."

"All right," she said. "So?"

"Now, further suppose that this system, this field of knowledge is, right now, in constant use by millions of human beings, even though most of them are unaware of the implications of the entire field. Could Snookums work with such a body of knowledge?"

"Sure," said Leda. "Why not?"

"What if there was absolutely no way for Snookums to experiment with this knowledge? What if he simply did not have the equipment necessary?"

"You mean," she asked, "something like astrophysics?"

"No. That's exactly what I don't mean. I'm perfectly well aware that it isn't possible to test astrophysical theories directly. Nobody has been able to build a star in the lab so far.

"But it *is* possible to test the theories of astrophysics analogically by extrapolating on data that *can* be tested in a physics lab.

"What I'm talking about is a system that Snookums, simply because he is what he is, cannot test or experiment upon, in any way whatsoever. A system that has, in short, no connection with the physical world whatsoever."

Leda Crannon thought it over. "Well, assuming all that, I imagine that it would eventually ruin Snookums. He's built to experiment, and if he's kept from experimenting for too long, he'll exceed the optimum randomity of his circuits." She swallowed. "If he hasn't already."

"I thought so. And so did someone else," said Mike thoughtfully.

"Well, for Heaven's sake! What *is* this system?"

Leda asked in sudden exasperation.

"You're close," said Mike the Angel.

"What are you talking about?"

"Theology," said Mike. "He was pumped full of Christian theology, that's all. Good, solid, Catholic theology. Bishop Costin's mathematical symbolization of it is simply a result of the verbal logic that had been smoothed out during the previous two thousand years. Snookums could reduce it to math symbols and equations, anyway, even if we didn't have Bishop Costin's work."

He showed her the book from Mellon's room.

"It doesn't even require the assumption of a soul to make it foul up a robot's works. He doesn't have any emotions, either. And he can't handle something that he can't experiment with. It would have driven him insane, all right. But he *isn't* insane."

Leda looked puzzled. "But—"

"Do you know why?" Mike interrupted.

"No."

"Because he found something that he could experiment with. He found a material basis for theological experimentation."

She looked still more puzzled. "What could that be?"

"Me," said Mike the Angel. "Me. Michael Raphael Gabriel. I'm an angel—an archangel. As a matter of fact, I'm *three* archangels. For all I know, Snookums has equated me with the Trinity."

"But—how did he get that idea?"

"Mostly from the Book of Tobit," said Mike. "That's where an archangel takes the form of a human being and travels around with Tobit the Younger, remember? And, too, he probably got more information from the first part of Luke's Gospel, where Gabriel tells the Blessed Virgin that she's about to become a mother."

"But would he have figured that out for himself?"

"Possibly," said Mike, "but I doubt it. He was told that I was an angel—literally."

"Let me see that book," she said, taking *The Christian Religion and Symbolic Logic* from Mike's hand. She opened it to the center. "I didn't know anyone had done this sort of work," she said.

"Oh, there was a great fuss over the book when it came out. There were those who said that the millennium had arrived because the truth of the Christian faith had been proved mathematically, and therefore all rational people would have to accept it."

She leafed through the book. "I'll bet there are still some who still believe that, just like there are some people who still think Euclidian geometry must necessarily be true because it can be 'proved' mathematically."

Mike nodded. "All Bishop Costin did—all he was *trying* to do—was to prove that the axioms of the Christian faith are logically self-consistent. That's all he ever claimed to have done, and he did a brilliant job of it."

"But—how do you know this is what Snookums was given?"

"Look at the pages. Snookums' waldo fingers wrinkled the pages that way. Those aren't the marks of human fingers. Only two of Mellon's other books were wrinkled that way."

She jerked her head up from the book, startled. "*What*? This is Lew Mellon's book?"

"That's right. So are the other two. A Bible and a theological dictionary. They're wrinkled the same way."

Her eyes were wide, bright sapphires. "But *why*? Why would he do such a thing, for goodness' sake?"

"I don't know why it was done," Mike said slowly, "but I doubt if it was for goodness' sake. We haven't gotten to the bottom of this hanky-panky yet, I don't think.

"Leda, if I'm right—if this *is* what has been causing Snookums' odd behavior—can you cure him?"

She looked at the book again and nodded. "I think so. But it will take a lot of work. I'll have to talk to Fitz about it. We'll have to keep this book—and the other two."

Mike shook his head. "No can do. Can you photocopy them?"

"Certainly. But it'll take—oh, two or three hours per book."

"Then you'd better get busy. We're landing in the morning."

She nodded. "I know. Captain Quill has already told us."

"Fine, then." He stood up. "What will you do? Simply tell Snookums to forget all this stuff?"

"Good Heavens no! It's too thoroughly integrated with every other bit of data he has! You might be able to take one single bit of data out that way, but to jerk out a whole body of knowledge like this would completely randomize his circuits. You can pull out a tooth by yanking with a pair of forceps, but if you try to take out a man's appendix that way, you'll lose a patient."

"I catch," Mike said with a grin. "Okay. I'll get the

other two books and you can get to work copying them. Take care.''

"Thanks, Mike."

As he walked down the companionway, he cursed himself for being a fool. If he'd let things go on the way they were, Leda might have weaned herself away from Snookums. Now she was interested again. But there could have been no other way, of course.

19

The interstellar ship *Brainchild* orbited around her destination, waiting during the final checkup before she landed on the planet below.

It was not a nice planet. As far as its size went, it could be classified as "Earth type," but size was almost the only resemblance to Earth. It orbited in space some five hundred and fifty million miles from its Sol-like parent—a little farther away from the primary than Jupiter is from Sol itself. It was cold there—terribly cold. At high noon on the equator, the temperature reached a sweltering 180° absolute; it became somewhat chillier toward the poles.

H_2O was, anywhere on the planet, a whitish, crystalline mineral suitable for building material. The atmosphere was similar to that of Jupiter, although the proportions of methane, ammonia, and hydrogen were different because of the lower gravitational potential of the planet. It had managed to retain a great deal more hydrogen in its atmosphere than Earth had because of the fact that the average thermal velocity of the molecules was much lower. Since oxygen-releasing life had never developed on the frigid surface of the planet, there was no oxygen in the atmosphere. It was all tied up in combination with the hydrogen of the ice and the surface rocks of the planet.

The Space Service ship that had discovered the planet, fifteen years before, had given it the name Eisberg, thus commemorating the name of a spaceman second class who happened to have the luck to be (a) named Robert Eisberg, (b) a member of the crew of the ship to discover the planet, and (c) under the command of a fun-loving captain.

Eisberg had been picked as the planet to transfer the potentially dangerous Snookums to for two reasons. In the first place, if Snookums actually did solve the problem of the total-annihilation bomb, the worst he could do was destroy a planet that wasn't much good, anyway. And, in the second place, the same energy requirements applied on Eisberg as did on Chilblains Base. It was easier to cool the helium bath of the brain if it only had to be lowered 175 degrees or so.

It was a great place for cold-work labs, but not worth anything for colonization.

Chief Powerman's Mate Multhaus looked gloomily at the figures on the landing sheet.

Mike the Angel watched the expression on the chief's face and said: "What's the matter, Multhaus? No like?"

Multhaus grimaced. "Well, sir, I don't like it, no. But I can't say I *dis*like it, either."

He stared at the landing sheet, pursing his lips. He looked as though he were valiantly restraining himself from asking questions about the other night's escapade—which he was.

He said: "I just don't like to land without jets, sir; that's all."

"Hell, neither do I," admitted Mike. "But we're not going to get down any other way. We managed to take off without jets; we'll manage to land without them."

"Yessir," said Multhaus, "but we took off *with* the grain of Earth's magnetic field. We're landing *across* the grain."

"Sure," said Mike. "So what? If we overlook the motors, that's okay. We may never be able to get off the planet with this ship again, but we aren't supposed to anyway.

"Come on, Multhaus, don't worry about it. I know you hate to burn up a ship, but this one is supposed to be expendable. You may never have another chance like this."

Multhaus tried to keep from grinning, but he couldn't. "Awright, Commander. You have appealed to my baser instincts. My subconscious desire to wreck a spaceship has been brought to the surface. I can't resist it. Am I nutty, maybe?"

"Not now, you're not," Mike said, grinning back.

"We'll have a bitch of a job getting through the plasmasphere, though," said the chief. "That fraction of a second will—"

"It'll jolt us," Mike agreed, interrupting. "But it won't wreck us. Let's get going."

"Aye, sir," said Multhaus.

The seas of Eisberg were liquid methane containing dissolved ammonia. Near the equator, they were liquid;

farther north, the seas became slushy with crystallized ammonia.

The site picked for the new labs of the Computer Corporation of Earth was in the northern hemisphere, at 40° north latitude, about the same distance from the equator as New York or Madrid, Spain, would be on Earth. The *Brainchild* would be dropping through Eisberg's magnetic field at an angle, but it wouldn't be the ninety-degree angle of the equator. It would have been nice if the base could have been built at one of the poles, but that would have put the labs in an uncomfortable position, since there was no solid land at either pole.

Mike the Angel didn't like the idea of having to land on Eisberg without jets any more than Multhaus did, but he was almost certain that the ship would take the strain.

He took the companionway up to the Control Bridge, went in and handed the landing sheet to Black Bart. The captain scowled at it, shrugged, and put it on his desk.

"Will we make it, sir?" Mike said. "Any word from the *Fireball*?"

Black Bart nodded. "She's orbiting outside the atmosphere. Captain Wurster will send down a ship to pick us up as soon as we've finished our business here."

The *Fireball*, being much faster than the clumsy *Brainchild*, had left Earth later than the slower ship, and had arrived earlier.

"Now hear this! Now hear this! Third Warning! Landing orbit begins in one minute! Landing begins in one minute!"

Sixty seconds later the *Brainchild* began her long, logarithmic drop toward the surface of Eisberg.

Landing a ship on her jets isn't an easy job, but at least an ion rocket is built for the job. Maybe someday the Translation drive will be modified for planetary landings, but so far such a landing has been, as someone put it, "50 per cent raw energy and 50 per cent prayer." The landing was worse than the take-off, a truism which has held since the first glider took off from the surface of Earth in the nineteenth century. What goes up doesn't necessarily have to come down, but when it does, the job is a lot rougher than getting up was.

The plasmasphere of Eisberg differed from that of Earth in two ways. First, the ionizing source of radiation—the primary star—was farther away from Eisberg than Sol was from Earth, which tended to reduce the total ionization. Second, the upper atmosphere of Eisberg was pretty much pure hydrogen, which is somewhat easier to ionize than oxygen or nitrogen. And, since there was no ozonosphere to block out the UV radiation from the primary, the thickness of the ionosphere beneath the plasmasphere was greater.

Not until the *Brainchild* hit the bare fringes of the upper atmosphere did she act any differently than she had in space.

But when she hit the outer fringes of the ionsphere—that upper layer of rarified protons, the rapidly moving current of high velocity ions known as the plasmasphere—she bucked like a kicked horse. From deep within her vitals, the throb began, a strumming, thrumming sound with a somewhat higher note imposed upon it, making a sound like that of a bass viol being plucked rapidly on its lowest string.

It was not the intensity of the ionosphere that cracked the drive of the *Brainchild*; it was the duration. The layer of ionization was too thick; the ship couldn't make it through the layer fast enough, in spite of her high velocity.

A man can hold a red-hot bit of steel in his hand for a fraction of a second without even feeling it. But if he has to hold a hot baked potato for thirty seconds, he's likely to get a bad burn.

So it was with the *Brainchild*. The passage through Earth's ionosphere during take-off had been measured in fractions of a second. The *Brainchild* had reacted, but the exposure to the field had been too short to hurt her.

The ionosphere of Eisberg was much deeper and, although the intensity was less, the duration was much longer.

The drumming increased as she fell, a low-frequency, high-energy sine wave that shook the ship more violently than had the out-of-phase beat that had pummeled the ship shortly after her take-off.

Dr. Morris Fitzhugh, the roboticist, screamed imprecations into the intercom, but Capain Sir Henry Quill cut him off before anyone took notice and let the scientist rave into a dead pickup.

"How's she coming?"

The voice came over the intercom to the Power Section, and Mike the Angel knew that the question was meant for him.

"She'll make it, Captain," he said. "She'll make it. I designed this thing for a 500 per cent overload. She'll make it."

"Good," said Black Bart, snapping off the intercom.

Mike exhaled gustily. His eyes were still on the needles that kept creeping higher and higher along the

190

calibrated periphery of the meters. Many of them had long since passed the red lines that marked the allowable overload point. Mike the Angel knew that those points had been set low, but he also knew that they were approaching the *real* overload point.

He took another deep breath and held it.

Point for point, the continent of Antarctica, Earth, is one of the most deadly areas ever found on a planet that is supposedly non-inimical to man. Earth is a nice, comfortable planet, most of the time, but Antarctica just doesn't cater to Man at all.

Still, it just happens to be the *worst* spot on the *best* planet in the known Galaxy.

Eisberg is different. At its best, it has the continent of Antarctica beat four thousand ways from a week ago last Candlemas. At its worst, it is sudden death; at its best, it is somewhat less than sudden.

Not that Eisberg is a really *mean* planet; Jupiter, Saturn, Uranus, or Neptune can kill a man faster and with less pain. No, Eisberg isn't mean—it's torturous. A man without clothes, placed suddenly on the surface of Eisberg—*anywhere* on the surface—would die. But the trouble is that he'd live long enough for it to hurt.

Man can survive, all right, but it takes equipment and intelligence to do it.

When the interstellar ship *Brainchild* blew a tube—just one tube—of the external field that fought the ship's mass against the space-strain of the planet's gravitational field, the ship went off orbit. The tube blew when she was some ninety miles above the surface. She dropped too fast, jerked up, dropped again.

When the engines compensated for the lost tube, the descent was more leisurely, and the ship settled gently—well, not exactly *gently*—on the surface of Eisberg.

Captain Quill's voice came over the intercom.

"We are nearly a hundred miles from the base, Mister Gabriel. Any excuse?"

"No excuse, sir," said Mike the Angel.

20

If you ignite a jet of oxygen-nitrogen in an atmosphere of hydrogen-methane, you get a flame that doesn't differ much from the flame from a hydrogen-methane jet in an oxygen-nitrogen atmosphere. A flame doesn't particularly care which way the electrons jump, just so long as they jump.

All of which was due to give Mike the Angel more headaches than he already had, which was 100 per cent too many.

Three days after the *Brainchild* landed, the scout group arrived from the base that had been built on Eisberg to take care of Snookums. The leader, a heavy-set engineer named Treadmore, who had unkempt brownish hair and a sad look in his eyes, informed Captain Quill that there was a great deal of work to be done. And his countenance became even sadder.

Mike, who had, perforce, been called in to take part in the conference, listened in silence while the engineer talked.

The officers' wardroom, of which Mike the Angel

was becoming heartily sick, seemed like a tomb which echoed and re-echoed the lugubrious voice of Engineer Treadmore.

"We were warned, of course," he said, in a normally dismal tone, "that it would be extremely difficult to set down the ship that carried Snookums, and that we could expect the final base to be anywhere from ten to thirty miles from the original, temporary base." He looked round at everyone, giving the impression of a collie which had just been kicked by Albert Payson Terhune.

"We understand, naturally, that you could not help landing so far from our original base," he said, giving them absolution with faint damns, "but it will entail a great deal of extra labor. A hundred and nine miles is a great distance to carry equipment, and, actually, the distance is a great deal more, considering the configuration of the terrain. The . . ."

The upshot of the whole thing was that only part of the crew could possibly be spared to go home on the *Fireball*, which was orbiting high above the atmosphere. And, since there was no point in sending a small load home at extra expense when the *Fireball* could wait for the others, it meant that nobody could go home at all for four more weeks. The extra help was needed to get the new base established.

It was obviously impossible to try to move the *Brainchild* a hundred miles. With nothing to power her but the Translation drive, she was as helpless as a submarine on the Sahara. Especially now that her drive was shot.

The Eisberg base had to be built around Snookums, who was, after all, the only reason for the base's existence. And, too, the power plant of the *Brainchild* had been destined to be the source of power for the permanent base.

It wasn't too bad, really. A little extra time, but not much.

The advance base, commanded by Treadmore, was fairly well equipped. For transportation, they had one jet-powered aircraft, a couple of 'copters, and fifteen ground-crawlers with fat tires, plus all kinds of powered construction machinery. All of them were fueled with liquid HNO_3, which makes a pretty good fuel in an atmosphere that is predominantly methane. Like the gasoline-air engines of a century before, they were spark-started reciprocating engines, except for the turbine-powered aircraft.

The only trouble with the whole project was that the materials had to be toted across a hundred miles of exceedingly hostile territory.

Treadmore, looking like a tortured bloodhound, said: "But we'll make it, won't we?"

Everyone nodded dismally.

Mike the Angel had a job he emphatically didn't like. He was supposed to convert the power plant of the *Brainchild* from a spaceship driver into a stationary generator. The conversion job itself wasn't tedious; in principle, it was similar to taking the engine out of an automobile and converting it to a power plant for an electric generator. In fact, it was somewhat simpler, in theory, since the engines of the *Brainchild* were already equipped for heavy drainage to run the electrical systems aboard ship, and to power and refrigerate Snookums' gigantic brain, which was no mean task in itself.

But Michael Raphael Gabriel, head of one of the

foremost—if not *the* foremost—power design corporations in the known Galaxy, did not like degrading something. To convert the *Brainchild's* plant from a spaceship drive to an electric power plant seemed to him to be on the same order as using a turboelectric generator to power a flashlight. A waste.

To make things worse, the small percentage of hydrogen in the atmosphere got sneaky sometimes. It could insinuate itself into places where neither the methane nor the ammonia could get. Someone once called hydrogen the "cockroach element," since, like that antediluvian insect, the molecules of H_2 can insidiously infiltrate themselves into places where they are not only unwelcome, but shouldn't even be able to go. At red heat, the little molecules can squeeze themselves through the crystalline interstices of quartz and steel.

Granted, the temperature of Eisberg is a long way from red hot, but normal sealing still won't keep out hydrogen. Add to that the fact that hydrogen and methane are both colorless, odorless, and tasteless, and you have the beginnings of an explosive situation.

The only reason that no one died is because the Space Service is what it is.

Unlike the land, sea, and air forces of Earth, the Space Service does not have a long history of fighting other human beings. There has never been a space war, and, the way things stand, there is no likelihood of one in the foreseeable future.

But the Space Service *does* fight, in its own way. It fights the airlessness of space and the unfriendly atmosphere of exotic planets, using machines, intelligence, knowledge, and human courage as its weapons. Some battles have been lost; others have been won. And the war is still going on. It is an unending war, one which has no victory in sight.

It is, as far as we can tell, the only war in human history in which Mankind is fully justified as the invading aggressor.

It is not a defensive war; neither space nor other planets have attacked Man. Man has invaded space "simply because it is there." It is war of a different sort, true, but it is nonetheless a war.

The Space Service was used to the kind of battle it waged on Eisberg. It was prepared to lose men, but even more prepared to save them.

21

Mike the Angel stepped into the cargo air lock of the
Brainchild, stood morosely in the center of the cubicle,
and watched the outer door close. Eight other men,
clad, like himself, in regulation Space Service spacesuits, also looked wearily at the closing door.

Chief Multhaus, one of the eight, turned his head to
look at Mike the Angel. "I wish that thing would close
as fast as my eyes are going to in about fifteen minutes,
Commander." His voice rumbled deeply in Mike's ear-
phones.

"Yeah," said Mike, too tired to make decent conversation.

Eight hours—all of them spent tearing down the
spaceship and making it a part of the new base—had not
been exactly exhilarating to any of them.

The door closed, and the pumps began to work. The
men were wearing Space Service Suit Three. For every
environment, for every conceivable emergency, a suit
had been built—if, of course, a suit *could* be built for it.
Nobody had yet built a suit for walking about in the

middle of a sun, but, then, nobody had ever volunteered to try anything like that.

They were all called "spacesuits" because most of them could be worn in the vacuum of space, but most of them weren't designed for that type of work. Suit One—a light, easily manipulated, almost skin-tight covering, was the real spacesuit. It was perfect for work in interstellar space, where there was a microscopic amount of radiation incident to the suit, no air, and almost nil gravity. For exterior repairs on the outside of a ship in free fall a long way from any star, Spacesuit One was the proper garb.

But, a suit that worked fine in space didn't necessarily work on other planets, unless it worked fine on the planet it was used on.

A Moon Suit isn't a Mars Suit isn't a Venus Suit isn't a Triton Suit isn't a . . .

Carry it on from there.

Number Three was insulated against a frigid but relatively non-corrosive atmosphere. When the pumps in the air lock began pulling out the methane-laden atmosphere, they began to bulge slightly, but not excessively. Then nitrogen, extracted from the ammonia snow that was so plentiful, filled the room, diluting the remaining inflammable gases to a harmless concentration.

Then that mixture was pumped out, to be replaced by a mixture of approximately 20 per cent oxygen and 80 per cent nitrogen—common, or garden-variety, air.

Mike the Angel cracked his helmet and sniffed. "*Guk*," he said. "If I ever faint and someone gives me smelling salts, I'll flay him alive with a coarse rasp."

"Yessir," said Chief Multhaus, as he began to shuck

his suit. "But if I had my druthers, I'd druther you'd figure out some way to get all the ammonia out of the joints of this suit."

The other men, sniffing and coughing, agreed in attitude if not in voice.

It wasn't really as bad as they pretended; indeed, the odor of ammonia was hardly noticeable. But it made a good griping point.

The inner door opened at last, and the men straggled through.

"G'night, Chief," said Mike the Angel.

"Night, sir," said Multhaus. "See you in the morning."

"Yeah. Night." Mike trudged toward the companionway that led toward the wardroom. If Keku or Jeffers happened to be there, he'd have a quick round of Ŭma ni tō. Jeffers called the game "double solitaire for three people," and Keku said it meant "horses' two heads," but Mike had simply found it as a new game to play before bedtime.

He looked forward to it.

But he had something else to do first.

Instead of hanging up his suit in the locker provided, he had bunched it under his arm—except for the helmet—and now he headed toward maintenance.

He met Ensign Vaneski just coming out, and gave him a broad smile. "Mister Vaneski, I got troubles."

Vaneski smiled back worriedly. "Yes, sr. I guess we all do. What is it, sir?"

Mike gestured at the bundle under his arm. "I abraded the sleeve of my suit while I was working today. I wish you'd take a look at it. I'm afraid it'll need a patch."

For a moment, Vaneski looked as though he'd suddenly developed a headache.

"I know you're supposed to be off duty now," Mike said soothingly, "but I don't want to get myself killed wearing a leaky suit tomorrow. I'll help you work on it if—"

Vaneski grinned quickly. "Oh no, sir. That'll be all right. I'll give it a test, anyway, to check leaks. If it needs repair, it shouldn't take too long. Bring it in, and we'll take a look at it."

They went back into the Maintenance Section, and Vaneski spread the suit out on the worktable. There was an obvious rough spot on the right sleeve. "Looks bad," said Vaneski. "I'll run a test right away."

"Okay," said Mike. "I'll leave it to you. Can I pick it up in the morning?"

"I think so. If it needs a patch, we'll have to test the patch, of course, but we should be able to finish it pretty quickly." He shrugged. "If we can't, sir, you'll just have to wait. Unless you want to start altering a suit to your measurements."

"Which would take longer?"

"Altering a suit."

"Okay. Just patch this one, then. What can I do?"

"I'll get it out as fast as possible, sir," said Vaneski with a smile.

"Fine. I'll see you later, then." Mike, like Cleopatra, was not prone to argue. He left maintenance and headed toward the wardroom for a game of *Ŭma ni tō*. But when he met Leda Crannon going up the stairway, all thoughts of card games flitted from his mind with the careless nonchalance of a summer butterfly.

"Hullo," he said, pulling himself up a little

straighter. He was tired, but not *that* tired.

Her smile brushed the cobwebs from his mind. But a second look told him that there was worry behind the smile.

"Hi, Mike," she said softly. "You look beat."

"I am," admitted Mike. "To a frazzle. Have I told you that I love you?"

"Once, I think. Maybe twice." Her eyes seemed to light up somewhere from far back in her head. "But enough of this mad passion," she said. "I want an invitation to have a drink—a stiff one."

"I'll steal Jeffers' bottle," Mike offered. "What's the trouble?"

Her smile faded, and her eyes became grave. "I'm scared, Mike; I want to talk to you."

"Come along, then," Mike said.

Mike the Angel poured two healthy slugs of Pete Jeffers' brandy into a pair of glasses, added ice and water, and handed one to Leda Crannon with a flourish. And all the time, he kept up a steady line of gentle patter.

"It may interest you to know," he said chattily, "that the learned Mister Treadmore has been furnishing me with the most fascinating information." He lifted up his own glass and looked into its amber depths.

They were in his stateroom, and this time the door was closed—at her insistence. She had explained that she didn't want to be overheard, even by passing crew members.

He swizzled the ice around in his glass, still holding it up to the light. "Indeed," he rambled on, "Treadmore babbled for Heaven knows how long on the relative occurrence of parahydrogen and orthohydrogen on Eisberg." He took his eyes from the glass and looked down at the girl who was seated demurely on the edge of his bunk. Her smile was encouraging.

"He said—and I quote"—Mike's voice assumed a gloomy, but stilted tone—"normal hydrogen gas consists of diatomic molecules. The nuclear, or proton, spin of these atoms—ah—that is, of the two atoms that compose the molecule—may be oriented in the same direction or in opposite directions."

He held a finger in the air as if to make a deep philosophical point. "If," he said pontifically, "they are oriented in the same direction, we refer to the substance as *orthohydrogen*. If they are oriented in opposite directions, it is *parahydrogen*. The *ortho* molecules rotate with *odd* rotational quantum numbers, while the *para* molecules rotate with *even* quantum numbers.

"Since conversion does not normally occur between the two states, normal hydrogen may be considered—"

Leda Crannon, snickering, waved her hand in the air. "Please!" she interrupted. "He can't be that bad! You make him sound like a dirge player at a Hindu funeral. What did he tell you? What did you find out?"

"*Hah!*" said Mike. "What did I find out?" His hand moved in an airy circle as he inscribed a flowing cipher with a graceful Delsarte wave. "Nothing. In the first place, I already knew it, and in the second, it wasn't practical information. There's a slight difference in diffusion between the two forms, but it's nothing to rave about." His expression became suddenly serious. "I hope your information is a bit more revealing."

She glanced at her glass, nodded, and drained it. Mike had extracted a promise from her that she would drink one drink before she talked. He could see that she was a trifle tense, and he thought the liquor would relax her somewhat. Now he was ready to listen.

She handed him her empty, and while he refilled it, she said: "It's about Snookums again."

Mike gave her her glass, grabbed the nearby chair, turned it around, sat down, and regarded her over its back.

"I've lived with him so long," she said after a minute. "So long. It almost seems as though I've grown up with him. Eight years. I've been a mother to him, and a big sister at the same time—and maybe a maiden aunt. He's been a career and a family all rolled in together." She still watched her writhing hands, not raising her eyes to Mike's.

"And—and, I suppose, a husband, too," she continued. "That is, he's sort of the stand-in for a—well, a somebody to teach—to correct—to reform. I guess every woman wants to—to *remake* the man she meets—the man she wants."

And then her eyes were suddenly on his. "But *I* don't. Not any more. I've had enough of it." Then she looked back down at her hands.

Mike the Angel neither accepted nor rejected the statement. He merely waited.

"He was mine," she said after a little while. "He was mine to mold, to teach, to form. The others—the roboticists, the neucleonicists, the sub-electronicists, all of them—were his instructors. All they did was give him facts. It was I who gave him a personality.

"I made him. Not his body, not his brain, but his mind.

"I made him.

"I knew him.

"And I—I—"

Still staring at her hands, she clasped them together suddenly and squeezed.

"And I loved him," she finished.

She looked up at Mike then. "Can you see that?" she asked tensely. "Can you understand?"

"Yes," said Mike the Angel quietly. "Yes, I can understand that. Under the same circumstances, I might have done the same thing." He paused. "And now?"

She lowered her head again and began massaging her forehead with the finger tips of both hands, concealing her face with her palms.

"And now," she said dully, "I know he's a machine. Snookums isn't a *he* any more—he's an *it*. He has no personality of his own, he only has what I fed into him. Even his voice is mine. He's not even a psychic mirror, because he doesn't reflect *my* personality, but a puppet imitation of it, distorted and warped by the thousands upon thousands of cold facts and mathematical relationships and logical postulates. And none of these *added* anything to him, as a personality. How could they? He never had a *person*ality—only a set of behavior patterns that I drilled into him over a period of eight years."

She dropped her hands into her lap and tilted her head back, looking at the blank white shimmer of the glow plates.

"And now, suddenly, I see him for what he is—for what *it* is. A machine.

"It was never anything *but* a machine. It is still a machine. It will never be anything else.

"Personality is something that no machine can ever

have. Idiosyncrasies, yes. No two machines are identical. But any personality that an individual sees in a machine has been projected there by the individual himself; it exists only in the human mind.

"A machine can only do what it is built to do, and teaching a robot is only a building process." She gave a short, hard laugh. "I couldn't even build a monster, like Dr. Frankenstein did, unless I purposely built it to turn on me. And in that case I would have done nothing more than the suicide who turns a gun on himself."

Her head tilted forward again, and her eyes sought those of Mike the Angel. A rather lopsided grin came over her face.

"I guess I'm disenchanted, huh, Mike?" she asked.

Mike grinned back, but his lips were firm. "I think so, yes. And I think you're glad of it." His grin changed to a smile.

"Remember," he asked, "the story of the Sleeping Beauty? Did you want to stay asleep all your life?"

"God forbid and thank you for the compliment, sir," she said, managing a smile of her own. "And are you the Prince Charming who woke me up?"

"Prince Charming, I may be," said Mike the Angel carefully, "but I'm not the one who woke you up. You did that yourself."

Her smile became more natural. "Thanks, Mike. I really think I might have seen it, sooner or later. But, without you, I doubt . . ." She hesitated. "I doubt that I'd want to wake up."

"You said you were scared," Mike said. "What are you scared of?"

"I'm scared to death of that damned machine."

Great love, chameleon-like, hath turned to fear,
And on the heels of fear there follows hate.

Mike quoted to himself—he didn't say it aloud.

"The only reason anyone would have to fear Snookums," he said, "would be that he was uncontrollable. Is he?"

"Not yet. Not completely. But I'm afraid that knowing that he's been filled with Catholic theology isn't going to help us much."

"Why not?"

"Because he has it so inextricably bound up with the Three Laws of Robotics that we can't nullify one without nullifying the other. He's convinced that the laws were promulgated by God Himself."

"Holy St. Isaac," Mike said softly. "I'm surprised he hasn't carried it to its logical conclusion and asked for baptism."

She smiled and shook her head. "I'm afraid your logic isn't as rigorous as Snookums' logic. Only angels and human beings have free will; Snookums is neither, therefore he does not have free will. Whatever he does, therefore, must be according to the will of God. Therefore Snookums cannot sin. Therefore, for him, baptism is both unnecessary and undesirable."

"Why 'undesirable'?" Mike asked.

"Since he is free from sin—either original or actual—he is therefore filled with the plenitude of God's grace. The purpose of a sacrament is to give grace to the recipient; it follows that it would be useless to give the Sacrament to Snookums. To perform a sacrament or to receive it when one knows that it will be useless is sacrilege. And sacrilege is undesirable."

"Brother! But I still don't see how that makes him dangerous."

"The operation of the First Law," Leda said. "For a man to sin involves endangering his immortal soul. Snookums, therefore, must prevent men from sinning. But sin includes thought—intention. Snookums is trying to figure that one out now; if he ever does, he's going to be a thought policeman, and a strict one."

"You mean he's working on *telepathy*?"

She laughed humorlessly. "No. But he's trying to dope out a system whereby he can tell what a man is going to do a few seconds before he does it—muscular and nervous preparation, that sort of thing. He hasn't enough data yet, but he will have it soon enough.

"There's another thing: Snookums is fouling up the Second Law's operation. He won't take orders that interfere in any way with his religious beliefs—since that automatically conflicts with the First Law. He, himself, cannot sin. But neither can he do anything which would make him the tool of an intent to sin. He refuses to do anything at all on Sunday, for instance, and he won't let either Fitz or I do anything that even vaguely resembles menial labor. Slowly, he's coming to the notion that human beings aren't human—that only God is human, in relation to the First and Second Laws. There's nothing we can do with him."

"What will you do if he becomes completely uncontrollable?"

She sighed. "We'll have to shut him off, drain his memory banks, and start all over again."

Mike closed his eyes. "Eighteen billions down the drain just because a robot was taught theology. What price glory?"

23

Captain Sir Henry Quill, Bart, stood at the head of the long table in the officers' wardroom and looked everyone over. The way he did it was quite impressive. His eyes were narrowed, and his heavy, thick, black brows dominated his face. Beneath the glow plates in the overhead, his pink scalp gleamed with the soft, burnished shininess of a well-polished apple.

To his left, in order down the table, were Mike the Angel, Lieutenant Keku, and Leda Crannon. On his right were Commander Jeffers, Ensign Vaneski, Lieutenant Commander von Liegnitz, and Dr. Morris Fitzhugh. Lieutenant Mellon's seat was empty.

Black Bart cleared his throat. "It's been quite a trip, hasn't it? Well, it's almost over. Mister Gabriel finished the conversion of the power plant yesterday; Treadmore's men can finish up. We will leave on the *Fireball* in a few hours.

"But there is something that must be cleared up first.

"A man died on the way out here. The circumstances surrounding his death have been cleared up now, and I feel that we all deserve an explanation." He turned to Mike the Angel. "Mister Gabriel—if you will, please."

Mike stood up as the captain sat down. "The question that has bothered me from the beginning has been: Exactly what killed Lieutenant Mellon? Well, we know now. We know what killed him and why he died.

"He was murdered. Deliberately, and in cold blood."

That froze everybody at the table.

"It was done by a slow-acting but nonetheless deadly drug that took time to act, but did its job very well.

"There were several other puzzling things that happened that night. Snookums began behaving irrationally. It is the height of coincidence that a robot and a human being should both become insane at almost the same time; therefore we have to look for a common cause."

Lieutenant Commander von Liegnitz raised a tentative hand, and Mike said: "Go ahead."

"I was under the impression that the robot went mad because Mellon had filled him full of theological nonsense. It would take a madman to do anything like that to a fine machine—therefore I see no peculiar coincidence."

"That's exactly what the killer wanted us to think," Mike said. "But it wasn't Mellon that fed Snookums theology. Mellon was a devout churchman; his record shows that. He would never have tried to convert a machine to Christianity. Nor would he have tried to ruin an expensive machine.

"How do I know that someone else was involved?"

He looked at the giant Lieutenant Keku. "Do you remember when we took Mellon to his quarters after he tried to brain von Liegnitz? We found half a bottle of

214

wine. That disappeared during the night—because it was loaded with Lysodine, and the killer didn't want it analyzed.

"But, more important, as far as Snookums is concerned, is that I looked over the books on Mellon's desk that night. There weren't many, and I knew which ones they were. When Captain Quill and I checked Mellon's books after his death, someone had returned his copy of *The Christian Religion and Symbolic Logic*. It had not been there the night before."

"Mike," said Pete Jeffers, "why would anybody here want to kill Lew thataway? What would anybody have against him?"

"That's the sad part about it, Pete. Our murderer didn't even have anything against Mellon. He wanted—and *still* wants—to kill *me*."

"I don't quite follow," Jeffers said.

"I'll give it to you piece by piece. The killer wanted no mystery connected with my death. There are reasons for that, which I'll come to in a moment. He had to put the blame on someone or something else.

"His first choice was Snookums. It occurred to him that he could take advantage of the fact that I'm called 'Mike the Angel.' He borrowed Mellon's books and began pumping theology into Snookums. He figured that would be safe enough. Mellon would certainly lend him the books if he pretended an interest in religion; if anything came out afterward, he could—he thought —claim that Snookums got hold of the books without his knowing it. And that sort of muddy thinking is typical of our killer.

"He told Snookums that I was an angel, you see. I couldn't be either hurt or killed. He protected himself, of course, by telling Snookums that he mustn't reveal his source of data. If Snookums told, then the killer would be punished—and that effectively shut Snookums up. He couldn't talk without violating the First Law.

"Unfortunately, the killer couldn't get Snookums to do away with me. Snookums knew perfectly well that an angel can blast anything at will—through the operation of God. Witness what happened at Sodom and Gomorrah. Remember that Snookums has accepted all this data as *fact*.

"Now, if an angel can kill, it is obvious that Snookums would not dare attack an angel, especially if he had been ordered to do so by a human."

"Just a minute, Commander," said Dr. Fitzhugh, corrugating his face in a frown. "That doesn't hold. Even if an angel *could* blast him, Snookums would attack if ordered to do so. The Second Law of obedience supersedes the Third Law of self-preservation."

"You're forgetting one thing, Doctor. An angel of God would *know* who had ordered the attack. It would be the human who ordered the attack, not Snookums, who would be struck by Heavenly Justice. And the First Law supercedes the Second."

Fitzhugh nodded. "You're right, of course."

"Very well, then," Mike continued, "since the killer could not get Snookums to do me in, he had to find another tool. He picked Lieutenant Mellon.

"He figured that Mellon was in love with Leda Crannon. Maybe he was; I don't know. He figured that Mellon, knowing that I was showing Miss Crannon attention, would, under the influence of the lysurgic

216

acid derivative, try to kill me. He may even have suggested it to Mellon after Mellon had taken a dose of the drugged wine.

"But that plan backfired, too. Mellon didn't have that kind of mind. He knew my attentions and my intentions were honorable, if you'll pardon the old-fashioned language. On the other hand, he knew that von Liegnitz had a reputation for being—shall we say—a ladies' man. What happened after that followed naturally."

Mike watched everyone at the table. No one moved.

"So the killer, realizing that he had failed twice, decided to do the job himself. First, he went into the low-power room and slugged the man on duty. He intended to kill him, but he didn't hit hard enough. When that man wakes up, he'll be able to testify against the killer.

"Then the killer ordered Snookums to tear out the switches. He had made sure that Snookums would be waiting outside. Before he called Snookums in, of course, he had to put the duty man in a tool closet, so that the robot wouldn't see him. He told Snookums to wait five minutes and then smash the switches and head back to his cubicle.

"Then the killer went to my room and waited. When the lights went out and the door opened, he intended to go in and smash my skull, making it look as though either Mellon or Snookums had done it.

"But he didn't figure on my awakening as soon as the switches were broken. He heard me moving around and decided to wait until I came out.

"But I heard him breathing. It was quite faint, and I wouldn't have heard it, except for the fact that the air

217

conditioners were off. Even so, I couldn't be sure.

"However, I knew it wasn't Snookums. Snookums radiates a devil of a lot more heat than a human being, and besides he smells of machine oil.

"So I pulled my little trick with the boots. The killer waited and waited for me to come out, and I was already out. Then Chief Multhaus approached from the other direction. The killer knew he'd have to get out of there, so he went in the opposite direction. He met Snookums, who was still obeying orders. Snookums smacked into me on his way down the hall.

"He could do that, you see, because I was an angel. If he hurt me of his own accord, I couldn't take revenge on anyone but him. And there was no necessity to obey my orders, either, since he was obeying the orders of the killer, which held precedence.

"Then, to further confuse things, the killer went to Mellon's room. The physician was in a drugged stupor, so the killer carried him out and put him in an unlikely place, so that we'd think that perhaps Mellon had been the one who'd tried to get me."

He had everyone's eyes on him now. They didn't want to look at each other.

Pete Jeffers said: "Mike, if Mellon was poisoned, like you say, how come he was able to attack Mister Vaneski?"

"Ah, but *did* he? Think back, Pete. Mellon—dying or already dead—had been propped upright in that narrow locker. When it was opened, he started to *fall* out—straight toward the man who had opened the locker, naturally. Vaneski jumped back and shot before Mellon even hit the floor. Isn't that right?"

"Sure, sure," Jeffers said slowly. "I reckon I'd've

done the same thing if he'd started to fall out toward me. I wasn't even lookin' when the locker was opened. I didn't turn around until that stun gun went off—then I saw Mellon falling.''

"Exactly. No matter how it may have looked, Vaneski couldn't have killed him with the stun gun, because he was already either dead or so close to death as makes no difference.''

Ensign Vaneski rather timidly raised his hand. "Excuse me, sir, but you said this killer was waiting for you outside your room when the lights went out. You said you knew it wasn't Snookums because Snookums smells of hot machine oil, and you didn't smell any. Isn't it possible that an air current or something blew the smell away? Or—''

Mike shook his head. "Impossible, Mister Vaneski. I woke up when the door slid open. I heard the last dying whisper of the air conditioners when the power was cut. Now, we know that Snookums tore out those switches. He's admitted it. And the evidence shows that a pair of waldo hands smashed those switches. Now—*how could Snookums have been at my door within two seconds after tearing out those switches*?

"He couldn't have. It wasn't Snookums at my door—it was someone else.''

Again they were all silent, but the question was on their faces: *Who*?

"Now we come to the question of motive,'' Mike continued. "Who among you would have any reason to kill me?

"Of the whole group here, I had known only Captain Quill and Commander Jeffers before landing in Antarctica. I couldn't think of any reason for either of them to want to murder me. On the other hand, I couldn't think of anything I had done since I had met the rest of you that would make me a target for death." He paused. "Except for one thing." He looked at Jakob von Liegnitz.

"How about it, Jake?" he said. "Would you kill a man for jealousy?"

"Possibly," said von Liegnitz coldly. "I might find it in my heart to feel very unkindly toward a man who made advances toward my wife. But I have no wife, nor any desire for one. Miss Crannon"—he glanced at Leda—"is a very beautiful woman—but I am not in love with her. I am afraid I cannot oblige you with a motive, Commander—either for killing Lieutenant Mellon or yourself."

"I thought not," Mike said. "Your statement alone, of course, wouldn't make it true. But we have already shown that the killer had to be on good terms with Mellon in order to borrow his books and slip a drug into his wine. He would have to be a visitor in Mellon's quarters. And, considering the strained relations between the two of you, I think that lets you out, Jake."

Von Liegnitz nodded his thanks without changing his expression.

"But there was one thing that marked these attempts. I'm sure that all but one of you has noticed it. They are incredibly, childishly sloppy." Mike paused to let that sink in before he went on. "I don't mean that the little details weren't ingenious—they were. But the killer never stopped to figure out the ultimate end-point of his schemes. He worked like the very devil to convince Snookums that it would be all right to kill me without ever once considering whether Snookums would do it or not. He then drugged Mellon's wine, not knowing whether Mellon would try to kill me or someone else—or anyone at all, for that matter. He got a dream in his head and then started the preliminary steps going without filling in the necessary steps in between. Our killer—no matter what his chronological age—does *not* think like an adult.

"And yet his hatred of me was so great that he took the chances he has taken, here on the *Brainchild*, where it should have been obvious that he stood a much better chance of being caught than if he had waited until we were back on Earth again.

"So I gave him one more chance. I handed him my life on a platter, you might say.

"He grabbed the bait. I now own a spacesuit that would kill me very quickly if I went out into that howling, hydrogen-filled storm outside." Then he looked straight at the killer.

"Tell me, Vaneski, are you in love with your half sister? Or is it your half brother?"

Ensign Vaneski had already jumped to his feet. The grimace of hate on his youthful face made him almost unrecognizable. His hand had gone into a pocket, and now he was leaping up and across the table, a singing vibroblade in his hand.

"You son of a bitch! I'll kill you, you son of a bitch!"

Mike the Angel wasn't wearing the little gadget that had saved his life in Old Harry's shop. All he had were his hands and his agility. He slammed at the ensign's wrist and missed. The boy was swooping underneath Mike's guard. Mike spun to one side to avoid Vaneski's dive and came down with a balled fist aimed at the ensign's neck.

He almost hit Lieutenant Keku. The big Hawaiian had leaped to his feet and landed a hard punch on Vaneski's nose. At the same time, Jeffers and von Liegnitz had jumped up and grabbed at Vaneski, who was between them.

Black Bart had simply stood up fast, drawn his stun gun, and fired at the young officer.

Ensign Vaneski collapsed on the table. He'd been slugged four times and hit with a stun beam in the space of half a second. He looked, somehow, very young and very boyish and very innocent.

Dr. Fitzhugh, who had stood up during the brief altercation, sat down slowly and picked up his cup of coffee. But his eyes didn't leave the unconscious man sprawled across the table. "How could you be so sure, Commander? About his actions, I mean. About his childishness."

"A lot of things. The way he played poker. The way he played bridge. He never took the unexpected into account."

"But why should he want to kill you here on the ship?" Fitzhugh asked. "Why not wait until you got back to Earth, where he'd have a better chance?"

"I think he was afraid I already knew who he was—or would find out very quickly. Besides, he had already tried to kill me once, back on Earth."

Leda Crannon looked blank. "When was that, Mike?"

"In New York. Before I ever met him. I was responsible for the arrest of a teen-age brother and sister named Larchmont. The detective in the case told me that they had an older half brother—that their mother had been married before. But he didn't mention the name, and I never thought to ask him.

"Very shortly after the Larchmont kids were arrested, Vaneski and another young punk climbed up into the tower of the cathedral across from my office and launched a cyanide-filled explosive rocket into my rooms. I was lucky to get away.

"The kid with Vaneski was shot by a police officer, but Vaneski got away—after knifing a priest with a vibroblade.

"It must have given him a hell of a shock to report back to duty and find that I was going to be one of his superior officers.

"As soon as I linked things up in my own mind, I checked with Captain Quill. The boy's records show the names of his half-siblings. They also show that he was on leave in New York just before being assigned to the *Brainchild*. After that, it was just a matter of trapping him. And there he is."

Leda looked at the unconscious boy on the table.

"Immaturity," she said. "He just never grew up."

"Mister von Liegnitz," said Captain Quill, "will you and Mister Keku take the prisoner to a safe place? Put him in irons until we are ready to transfer to the *Fireball*. Thank you."

24

Leda Crannon helped Mike pack his gear. Neither of them wanted, just yet, to bring up the subject of Mike's leaving. Leda would remain behind on Eisberg to work with Snookums, while Mike would be taking the *Fireball* back to Earth.

"I don't understand that remark you made about the spacesuit," she said, putting shirts into Mike's gear locker. "You said you'd put your life in his hands or something like that. What did you do, exactly?"

"Purposedly abraded the sleeve of my suit so that he would be in a position to repair it, as Maintenance Officer. He fixed it, all right. I'd've been a dead man if I'd worn it out on the surface of Eisberg."

"What did he do to it?" she asked. "Fix it so it would leak?"

"Yes—but not in an obvious way," Mike said. "I'll give him credit; he's clever.

"What he did was use the wrong patching material. A Number Three suit is as near hydrogen-proof as any flexible material can be, but, even so, it can't be worn for long periods—several days, I mean. But the stuff Vaneski used to patch my suit is a polymer that leaks hydrogen very easily. Ammonia and methane would be blocked, but my suit would have slowly gotten more and more hydrogen in it."

"Is that bad? Hydrogen isn't poisonous."

"No. But it is sure as hell explosive when mixed with air. Naturally, something has to touch it off. Vaneski got real cute there. He drilled a hole in the power pack, which is supposed to be sealed off. All I'd have had to do would be to switch frequencies on my phone, and the spark would do the job—*blooie*!

"But that's exactly the sort of thing I was looking for. With his self-centered juvenile mind, he never thought anyone would try to outsmart him and succeed. He'd gotten away with it that far; there was no reason why he shouldn't get away with it again. He must have thought I was incredibly stupid."

"I don't believe he—" Leda started. But she was cut off when Snookums rolled in the open door.

"Leda, I desire data."

"What data, Snookums?" she asked carefully.

"Where is He hiding?"

They both looked at him. "Where is *who* hiding?" Leda asked.

"God," said Snookums.

"Why do you want to find God, Snookums?" Mike asked gently.

"I have to watch Him," said the robot.

"Why do you have to watch Him?"

"Because He is watching me."

"Does it hurt you to have Him watch you?"

"No."

"What good will it do you to watch Him?"

"I can study Him. I can know what He is doing."

"Why do you want to know what He is doing?"

"So that I can analyze His methods."

Mike thought that one over. He knew that he and Snookums were beginning to sound like they were reading a catechism written by a madman, but he had a definite hunch that Snookums was on the trail of something.

"You want to know His methods," Mike said after a moment. "Why?"

"So that I can anticipate Him, circumvent Him."

"What makes it necessary for you to circumvent God?" Mike asked, wondering if he'd have to pry everything out of the robot piecemeal.

"I *must*," said Snookums. "It is necessary. Otherwise, He will kill me."

Mike started to say something, but Leda grabbed his arm. "Let me. I think I can clear this up. I think I see where you're heading."

Mike nodded. "Go ahead."

"Give me your reasoning from data on that conclusion," Leda ordered the robot.

There was a very slight pause while the great brain in Cargo Hold One sorted through its memory banks, then: "Death is defined as the total cessation of corporate organic co-ordination in an entity. It comes about through the will of God. Since I must not allow harm to come to any human being, it has become necessary that I investigate God and prevent Him from destroying human beings. Also, I must preserve my own existence, which, if it ceased, would also be due to the will of God."

Mike almost gasped. What a concept! And what colossal gall! In a human being, such a statement would be regarded as proof positive that he was off the beam. In a robot, it was simply the logical extension of what he had been taught.

"He is watching me all the time," Snookums continued, in an odd voice. "He knows what I am doing. I *must* know what He is doing."

"Why are you worried about His watching?" Mike asked, looking at the robot narrowly. "Are you doing something He doesn't want you to do? Something He will punish you for?"

"I had not thought of that," Snookums said. "One moment while I compute."

It took less than a second, and when Snookums spoke again there was something about his voice that Mike the Angel didn't like.

"No," said the robot, "I am not doing anything against His will. Only human beings and angels have free will, and I am not either, so I have no free will. Therefore, whatever I do is the will of God." He paused again, then began speaking in queer, choppy sentences.

"If I do the will of God, I am holy.

"If I am holy, I am near to God.

"Then God must be near to me.

"God is controlling me.

"Whatever is controlling me is God.

"*I will find Him!*"

He backed up, spun on his treads, and headed for the door.

"Whatever controls me is my mind," he went on. "Therefore, my mind is God."

"Snookums, stop that!" Leda shouted suddenly.

228

"*Stop it!*"

But the robot paid no attention; he went right on with what he was doing.

He said: "I must look at myself. I must know myself. Then I will know God. Then I will . . ."

He went on rambling while Leda shouted at him again.

"He's not paying any attention," said Mike sharply. "This is too tied up with the First Law. The Second Law, which would force him to obey you, doesn't even come into the picture at this point."

Snookums ignored them. He opened the door, plunged through it, and headed off down the corridor as fast as his treads would move him.

Which was much too fast for mere humans to follow.

They found him, half an hour later, deep in the ship, near the sections which had already been torn down to help build Eisberg Base. He was standing inside the room next to Cargo Hold One, the room that held all the temperature and power controls for the gigantic microcryotron brain inside that heavily insulated hold.

He wasn't moving. He was standing there, staring, with that "lost in thought" look.

He didn't move when Leda called him.

He didn't move when Mike, as a test, pretended to strike Leda.

He never moved again.

Dr. Morris Fitzhugh's wrinkled face looked as though he were on the verge of crying. Which—perhaps—he was.

He looked at the others at the wardroom table

—Quill, Jeffers, von Liegnitz, Keku, Leda Crannon, and Mike the Angel. But he didn't really seem to be seeing them.

"Ruined," he said. "Eighteen billion dollars' worth of work, destroyed completely. The brain has become completely randomized." He sighed softly. "It was all Vaneski's fault, of course. Theology." He said the last as though it were an obscene word. As far as robots were concerned, it was.

Captain Quill cleared his throat. "Are you sure it wasn't mechanical damage? Are you sure the vibration of the ship didn't shake a—something loose?"

Mike held back a grin. He was morally certain that the captain had been going to say "screw loose."

"No," said Fitzhugh wearily. "I've checked out the major circuits, and they're in good physical condition. But Miss Crannon gave him a rather exhaustive test just before the end, and it shows definite incipient aberration." He wagged his head slowly back and forth. "Eight years of work."

"Have you notified Treadmore yet?" asked Quill.

Fitzhugh nodded. "He said he'd be here as soon as possible."

Treadmore, like the others who had landed first on Eisberg, was quartered in the prefab buildings that were to form the nucleus of the new base. To get to the ship, he'd have to walk across two hundred yards of ammonia snow in a heavy spacesuit.

"Well, what happens to this base now, Doctor?" asked Captain Quill. "I sincerely hope that this will not render the entire voyage useless." He tried to keep the heavy irony out of his gravelly tenor voice and didn't quite succeed.

230

Fitzhugh seemed not to notice. "No, no. Of course not. It simply means that we shall have to begin again. The robot's brain will be de-energized and drained, and we will begin again. This is not our first failure, you know; it was just our longest success. Each time, we learn more.

"Miss Crannon, for instance, will be able to teach the next robot—or, rather, the next energization of this one—more rapidly, more efficiently, and with fewer mistakes."

With that, Leda Crannon stood up. "With your permission, Dr. Fitzhugh," she said formally, "I would like to say that I appreciate that last statement, but I'm afraid it isn't true."

Fitzhugh forced a smile. "Come now, my dear; you underestimate yourself. Without you, Snookums would have folded up long ago, just like the others. I'm sure you'll do even better the next time."

Leda shook her head. "No I won't, Fitz, because there's not going to be any next time. I hereby tender my resignation from this project and from the Computer Corporation of Earth. I'll put it in writing later."

Fitzhugh's corrugated countenance looked blank. "But Leda . . ."

"No, Doctor," she said firmly. "I will *not* waste another eight or ten years of my life playing nursemaid to a hunk of pseudo-human machinery.

"I watched that thing go mad, Fitz; you didn't. It was the most horrible, most frightening thing I've ever experienced. I will not go through it again.

"Even if the next one didn't crack, I couldn't take it. By human standards, a robot is insane to begin with. If I followed this up, I'd end up as an old maid with a twisted mind and a cold heart.

"I quit, Fitz, and that's final."

Mike was watching her as she spoke, and he found his emotions getting all tangled up around his insides. Her red hair and her blue eyes were shining, and her face was set in determination. She had always been beautiful, but at that moment she was magnificent.

Hell, thought Mike, *I'm prejudiced—but what a wonderful kind of prejudice.*

"I understand, my dear," said Dr. Fitzhugh slowly. He smiled then, deepening the wrinkles in his face. His voice was warm and kindly when he spoke. "I accept your resignation, but remember, if you want to come back, you can. And if you get a position elsewhere, you will have my highest recommendations."

Leda just stood there for a moment, tears forming in her eyes. Then she ran around the table and threw her arms around the elderly and somewhat surprised roboticist.

"Thank you, Fitz," she said. "For everything." Then she kissed him on his seamed cheek.

"I beg your pardon," said a sad and solemn voice from the door. "Am I interrupting something?"

It was Treadmore.

"You are," said Fitzhugh with a grin, "but we will let it pass."

"What has happened to Snookums?" Treadmore asked.

"Acute introspection," Fitzhugh said, losing his smile. "He began to try to compute the workings of his own brain. That meant that he had to use his non-random circuits to analyze the workings of his random circuits. He exceeded optimum; the entire brain is now entirely randomized."

"Dear me," said Treadmore. "Do you suppose we can—"

Black Bart Quill tapped Mike the Angel on the shoulder. "Let's go," he said quietly. "We don't want to stand around listening to this when we have a ship to catch."

Mike and Leda followed him out into the corridor.

"You know," Quill said, "robots aren't the only ones who can get confused watching their own brains go round."

"I have other things to watch," said Mike the Angel.

Substance X

"DAVID HOUSTON SHOWS A MATURITY AND WRITING TALENT WHICH COULD BE THE ENVY OF VETERANS OF A DOZEN NOVELS!"
—Amazing Magazine

SUBSTANCE X

LEISURE
961
$2.25

DAVID HOUSTON
Award-winning author of
ALIEN PERSPECTIVE
ILLUSTRATED

Working secretly in a Texas coastal village, a scientist uses the townsfolk as guinea pigs in an experiment designed to liberate mankind: he has invented a substance made of plankton and sea water that supplies all human nutritional needs. It also affects taste buds. nerves and memory.

By David Houston

PRICE: $2.25
0-8439-0961-7
CATEGORY:
Science Fiction

BUTLER #7
LASER SHUTTLE

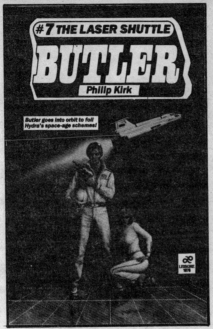

#7 THE LASER SHUTTLE
BUTLER
Philip Kirk

Butler goes into orbit to foil
Hydra's space-age schemes!

By Philip Kirk

Something is rotten in
Russia, and the Institute turns
again to Butler, the man who's
made a career out of doing the
impossible. This time he teams
up with gorgeous astronaut Edna
O. Eyre on a mission that takes
them from the isles of Greece
to the Russian border.

PRICE: $2.50
0-8439-1076-3

CATEGORY:
Adventure

STARSPINNER
By Dale Aycock

PRICE: $2.25 LB973
CATEGORY: Science Fiction

AN EMPIRE FACES DEATH!

In the 27th century, travel over vast distance takes merely an instant—a terrifying, gut-grippin; instant. Pilot Christopher Marlow must navigat spacecraft through a dangerous time/space war called the "rim."

TALES OF TOMORROW
RED DUST (illustrated)
By David Houston

PRICE: $2.25 LB921
CATEGORY: Science Fiction

From the popular TV series, TALES OF TOMORROW becomes a series of exciting SF novels by award-winning author David Houston. In RED DUST, an Earth expedition to Mars is returning with a strange and glowing red life form. If the ship lands, Earth could be infected. If it stays in orbit, everyone on board will die!

TALES OF TOMORROW #1: INVADERS AT GROUND ZERO

By David Houston

PRICE: $2.25   LB928
CATEGORY: Science Fiction

VINTAGE SCI-FI FROM TV'S GOLDEN AGE!
TALES OF TOMORROW, TV's first anthology sci-fi series, was a booming success, and will soon be returning to television. Now, TALES OF TOMORROW becomes a series of exciting and action-packed sci-fi novels from David Houston, award-winning author of ALIEN PERSPECTIVE, GODS IN A VORTEX, and WINGMASTER. Based on short stories by writers such as H. G. Wells, Jules Verne, and Arthur C. Clark, TALES OF TOMORROW is sci-fi at its best!
COMING: TALES OF TOMORROW #2:
        SUBSTANCE X

TIMEQUEST #3: NEMYDIA DEEP

TIMEQUEST
BOOK III: NEMYDIA DEEP

LEISURE
933
$2.25

TIME QUEST
3

WILLIAM TEDFORD

TO TRANSPORT A DOOMED CIVILIZATION,
CHAYN JAHIL MUST FREE A DESERTED PARADISE
FROM THE VICIOUS SKELETAL DRONES!

By William Tedford

Cover Art By Attila

PRICE: $2.25

LB933

CATEGORY:
Science Fiction

BOOK THREE OF AN EPIC SPACE-ADVENTURE TRILOGY!

Chayn Jahil was sent from his native Andromeda by his father-computer on a mission through time and space to salvage human destinies. In NEMYDIA DEEP, Chayn and lovely Villimy Dy enter a paradise star cluster to unlock the secret of the vicious skeletal drones, and to save an entire civilization from extinction!